JOSEPH ROTH (1894–1939) was the great elegist of the cosmopolitan, tolerant and doomed Central European culture that flourished in the dying days of the Austro-Hungarian Empire. Born into a Jewish family in Galicia, on the eastern edge of the empire, he was a prolific political journalist and novelist. On Hitler's assumption of power, he was obliged to leave Germany for Paris, where he died in poverty a few years later. His books include *What I Saw*, *Job*, *The String of Pearls*, *The Radetzky March* and *The Emperor's Tomb*, all published by Granta Books.

Praise for Joseph Roth:

'Read all his books, his stories, his observations and wonder at the intelligence, natural poetry and humanity of a gifted and candid master storyteller' Eileen Battersby, *Irish Times*

'Joseph Roth is one of the greatest European writers of the 20th century, [who] is finally beginning to gain the audience and the serious attention he deserves' *Evening Standard*

'Roth's writing is unambiguous, direct, and suffused with period detail' *Scotland on Sunday*

'Roth was a great storyteller. Small miracles of timing and mood occur on each page' *Daily Telegraph*

'Reading him is like reading a prophet: provocative, discomforting, full of insight and foreboding' *Tribune*

'When you dip into Roth you will soon want to immerse yourself completely' *Spectator*

'A clean, unfussy style ... Roth's humanity shines through.' *Irish Independent*

JOB

*The Story of
a Simple Man*

Joseph Roth

Translated by
Dorothy Thompson

GRANTA

Granta Publications, 12 Addison Avenue, London W11 4QR

First published in Great Britain by William Heinemann Ltd 1933
Previously published by Granta Books 2000
This edition published by Granta Books 2013

Originally published as *Hiob, Roman eines einfachen Mannes*
in 1930

A CIP catalogue record for this book
is available from the British Library.

3 5 7 9 10 8 6 4 2

ISBN 978 1 84708 616 7

Typeset in New Baskerville by M Rules

Printed and bound by CPI Group (UK) Ltd, Croydon, CR0 4YY

Part One

QUESTIONS FROM MARIA....

① RELATIONSHIP BETWEEN MENDEL + GOD?

② RELATIONSHIP Between Mendel + his wife?

③ What is the impact of their son?

—

DOES MENDEL BELIEVE IN MIRACLES AT THE BEGINNING?
DOES HE STOP BELIEVING IN GOD THROUGHOUT THE BOOK.

CLU BOOK DISCUSSION

FRAN:

*GOD'S FAITHFULNESS → EVEN WHEN MENDEL LEAVES.
HIS SON IS GIVEN BACK EVEN MORE BECAUSE
THEY DID THE ONE THING GOD ASKED THEM NOT TO.
AND YET HE STILL REMAINS FAITHFUL

JOHNOTHAN LIEDL:

* Fear guides a lot of Mendels life, it has a crippling effect

LUCIA:

The moment when Mendel deny's God the most
is when the presense of God has become so neal.
His anger became a dialogue that made God neal.

M. PIETRO:

The entire book is a cry → a cry to be forgiven.
Mendel needs to see his Son again for
this reason, to know that he is forgiven and that
God has a face.

I

MANY YEARS AGO there lived in Zuchnow in Russia, a man named Mendel Singer. He was pious, God-fearing, and ordinary, an entirely commonplace Jew. He practised the simple profession of a teacher. In his house, which was merely a roomy kitchen, he instructed children in the knowledge of the Bible. He taught with honourable zeal and without notable success. Hundreds of thousands before him had lived and taught as he did.

As insignificant as his nature was his pale face. A full beard of ordinary black framed it. The mouth was hidden by the beard. The eyes were large, black, dull, and half veiled by heavy lids. On the head sat a cap of black silk rep, a stuff out of which unfashionable and cheap cravats are sometimes made. His body was stuck into the customary half-long Jewish caftan of the country, the skirts of which flapped when Mendel Singer hurried through the street and struck with a hard regular tact like the beat of wings against the shafts of his high leather boots.

Singer seemed to have little time and a lot of pressing engagements. True, his life was always hard and at times even a torment to him. A wife and three children had to be clothed and fed. (She was carrying a fourth.) God had given fertility to his loins, equanimity to his heart, and poverty to his hands. They had no gold to weigh and no bank-notes to count. Nevertheless his life flowed along like a poor little brook between bare banks. Every morning Mendel thanked God for his sleeping, for his awakening, and for the dawning day. When the sun went down he said his prayers once again. When the first stars began to sparkle, he prayed for the third time, and before he laid himself down to sleep he whispered a hurried prayer, with tired but zealous lips. His sleep was dreamless, his conscience was pure, his soul was chaste.

He had nothing to regret, and he coveted nothing. He loved the woman, his wife, and took delight in her flesh. His two small sons, Jonas and Shemariah, he beat when they were disobedient, but the youngest, his daughter Miriam, he was constantly caressing. She had his black hair and his black, soft, and indolent eyes. Her limbs were tender and fragile. A young gazelle.

He instructed twelve six-year-old scholars in the reading and memorizing of the Bible. Each of the twelve brought him twenty kopeks every Friday. This was Mendel Singer's only income. He was just thirty years old but his chances of earning more were small, perhaps non-existent. When the students grew older they would go to other, wiser teachers. Living became dearer from year to year. The crops were always poorer and poorer. The carrots diminished, the eggs were hollow, the potatoes froze, the soup was watery, the carp thin, the pike short, the ducks lean, the geese tough, and the chickens amounted to nothing.

Thus sounded the complaints of Deborah, the wife of Mendel Singer. She was a woman; sometimes she seemed possessed. She looked askance at the possessions of the well-to-do and envied merchants their profits. In her eyes Mendel Singer was inconsiderable. She blamed him for the children, for her pregnancy, for the high prices, for his poor fees, and sometimes, even, for the bad weather. On Friday she scrubbed the floor until it was yellow as saffron. Her broad shoulders bobbed up and down in an even rhythm; her strong hands rubbed the length and breadth of each single board; and her finger-nails sought in the cracks between the boards, scratched out the black dirt, and destroyed it with splashes of water from her pail. She crept through the bare blue-whitewashed room like a broad, mighty, and movable mountain. Outside, before the door, she aired the furniture, the brown wooden bed, the sacks of straw, the scrubbed deal table, two long, narrow benches, each a horizontal board nailed on two vertical ones. As soon as the first twilight misted the windows, Deborah lighted the candles in the plated candlesticks, threw her hands over her face, and prayed.

Her husband came home, in silky black; the floor shone up at him, yellow as melted sunshine; his countenance shimmered whiter than usual, and blacker than on weekdays gleamed his beard. He sat down, sang a little song, and then parents and children sipped their soup, smiled at the plates, and spoke no word. Warmth rose in the room. It exuded from the pots, from the platters, and from their bodies. The cheap candles in the plated candlesticks could not stand it, they began to bend. Tallow dropped upon the red-and-blue checked tablecloth, and became encrusted immediately. The window was thrown open; the candles manfully took hold of themselves and burned peacefully to the end. The children laid themselves upon the straw sacks, near the stove, but the parents sat awhile and gazed with troubled solemnity into the last blue flames which rose up out of the sockets of the candlesticks and wavered back, a fountain-play of fire. The tallow smouldered, thin blue threads of smoke drew upward towards the ceiling from the embers of wick. 'Ah!' sighed the woman. 'Do not sigh,' warned Mendel Singer. They were silent. 'Let us sleep, Deborah,' he commanded. And they began to murmur the nightly prayer.

At the end of each week the Sabbath dawned thus, with silence, candles, and song. Twenty-four hours later the Sabbath sank into night; the grey procession of weekdays began, a weary cycle.

On a hot midsummer day, Deborah was confined. Her first cries pierced the sing-song of the twelve studying children. They all went home for a week's vacation.

Mendel got a new child, a fourth, a boy. Eight days later he was circumcised and named Menuchim.

Menuchim had no cradle. He swung in a basket of braided reeds, secured to a hook in the middle of the ceiling, like a chandelier. From time to time Mendel Singer pushed the hanging basket with a gentle, not unloving finger, and immediately it began to swing back and forth. But sometimes nothing would still the infant's desire to whimper and cry. His voice croaked over the voices of the twelve studying children, an ugly and profane noise above the Bible's holy verses. Deborah stood on a footstool and lifted the infant down. White, swollen, and colossal, her breast flowed from her open blouse and drew the glances of the boys irresistibly. All present seemed to suckle at Deborah. Her own three older children stood about her, jealous and greedy; the room became still. One heard the smacking of the infant.

Days drew themselves out into weeks, weeks grew into months, twelve months made a year. Menuchim still drank his mother's thin clear milk. She could not wean him. In the thirteenth month of his life he began to make faces and to groan like an animal, to breathe hastily and to gasp in an extraordinary fashion. His great skull hung heavy as a pumpkin on his thin neck. His broad brow was criss-crossed with folds and wrinkles like a crumpled parchment. His legs were crooked and lifeless, like two wooden bows. His meagre little arms twitched and fidgeted. His mouth stammered ridiculous noises. When he got an attack he was taken from his cradle and given a good shaking until his face was blue and his breath almost failed. Then he slowly recovered. Little sacks of tea-leaves were laid upon his poor breast and a poultice of herbs was bound about his thin neck. 'It's nothing,' said his father. 'Just growing-pains.' 'Sons take after the brothers of their mother. My brother had it five years!' said the mother. 'He'll grow out of it!' said the others.

Then one day smallpox broke out in the town; the authorities ordered vaccination, and the doctors forced their way into the houses of the Jews. Many hid themselves, but Mendel Singer, the righteous, fled before no punishment of God. Resigned, he even accepted the vaccination.

It was a warm sunny morning when the commission came through Mendel's street. In the row of Jewish houses Mendel's was the last. Accompanied by a policeman, who carried a big book under his arm, Dr. Soltysiuk went to perform the vaccination, a fluttering, blond moustache in his brown face, a gold-rimmed pince-nez on his reddened nose, taking long steps, creaking in his yellow leather leggings. Because of the heat his coat hung on his shoulders over his blue smock so that its sleeves looked like an extra pair of arms, also prepared to do vaccinations. Thus came Dr. Soltysiuk into the streets of the Jews. About him resounded the lamentations of women and the howls of children who had not been able to hide themselves. The policeman pulled women and children out of deep cellars and down from high attics, out of narrow closets and great straw baskets. The sun brooded, the doctor sweated. He had to vaccinate no less than one hundred and seventy-six Jews; for each who escaped and could not be reached, he thanked God in his heart. When he reached the fourth of the little blue-whitewashed houses, he winked at the policeman not to search too zealously. The farther the doctor went, the louder swelled the screaming. It floated before his steps. The howling of those who were still afraid united with the curses of those who were already inoculated. Weary and distrait, he sank with a heavy groan upon the bench in Mendel's kitchen and asked for a glass of water. His glance fell upon little Menuchim. He lifted the cripple and said: 'He will be an epileptic.' He planted anxiety in the father's heart. 'All children have their periods,' put in the mother. 'It's not that,' insisted the doctor. 'But perhaps I could cure him. There is life in his eyes.'

He wanted to take the little one to the hospital immediately. Deborah was ready. 'They will cure him free,' she said. But Mendel replied: 'Be still, Deborah! No doctor can cure him, if God does not will it. Should he grow up among Russian children? Never hear a holy word? Eat milk with meat and chickens roasted in butter, the way people get them in the hospital? We are poor, but I will not sell Menuchim's soul just because he can be cured free. One is not healed in strange hospitals.'

Like a hero Mendel held out his scraggy white arm to be vaccinated. But he would not give Menuchim away. He decided to beseech God's help for his youngest and to fast twice in the week, Mondays and Thursdays.

Deborah undertook pilgrimages to the cemetery; she called upon the bones of her ancestors to plead her cause before the Almighty. Thus would Menuchim become well and no epileptic.

Nevertheless, after the hour of the vaccination, fear hung over the house of Mendel Singer like a monster, and care blew steadily through their hearts like a hot, piercing wind. Deborah would sigh and her husband did not reprove her. When she prayed, she held her face buried longer than usual in her hands, as though she created her own night in which to bury her fears, and her own darkness in which to find peace. For she believed, as it stands written, that God's light shines in the darkness and His goodness illumines the black night.

The older children grew and grew; their healthiness sounded an evil warning in the ears of the mother as though it were inimical to Menuchim. It was as though the healthy children drew strength from the sickly one, and Deborah hated their noisiness, their red cheeks, their straight limbs. She pilgrimaged to the cemetery in rain and shine. She struck her head against the mossy sandstone which grew up from the bones of her father and mother. She called upon the dead whose quiet comforting answer she thought she heard. On the way home she trembled with the hope that she would find her son cured. She neglected her duties at the hearth; the soup ran over, the earthen pots cracked, the pans rusted, the shimmering green glasses splintered with a sharp report, the chimney of the oil lamp was clouded with soot, the wick charred away to a miserable stump, the dirt of many soles and many weeks lay thick upon the boards of the floor, the dripping melted in the pots, the buttons withered from the shirts of the children like leaves before the winter.

One day, a week before the high holy days (the summer had turned into rain and the rain sought to turn into snow), Deborah packed her son in a basket, laid a blanket over him, put him on the cart of the driver Sameshkin, and journeyed to Kluczysk, where the Rabbi lived. The boardseat lay loosely upon the straw and slid out of place with every movement of the wagon. Deborah had to hold it down by the main weight of her body. It was a living thing; it wanted to hop about. The narrow winding streets were covered with a silver-grey mud. The high boots of the passersby sank into it, and the cartwheels disappeared to the hubs. Rain veiled the fields, dispersed the smoke over the isolated huts, pounded with endless patience everything firm that it struck – the limestone, which here and there grew out of the earth like a white tooth; the sawed-up logs at the edges of the road; the aromatic boards piled one upon another before the entrance to the saw-mill; the shawl on Deborah's head; and the woollen blanket under which Menuchim lay buried. No drop must wet him.

Deborah reckoned that she still had four hours to go; if the rain did not stop, she would have to wait in an inn and dry the blanket, drink tea, and eat the dampened poppy-seed pretzels she had brought with her. That could cost five kopeks, five kopeks, which one did not throw about carelessly. God Himself could see that; it stopped raining. Above flying rags of cloud a blurred sun shone pale for barely an hour; then it finally sank in a new and deeper twilight.

Black night occupied Kluczysk, when Deborah arrived. Many bewildered people had already come to see the Rabbi. Kluczysk consisted of a few thousand low thatched and shingled houses and a market-place more than a half-mile square which looked like a dry lake wreathed round with buildings. The conveyances which stood around in it were like derelict vessels, tiny and meaningless, lost in the surrounding vastness. The unharnessed horses whinnied beside the carts and trod the sticky mire with tired smacking hoofs. A few men wandered through this circle of night with wavering yellow lanterns, to fetch a forgotten blanket or clattering dishes with provisions for the journey.

Round about, among the thousand little houses, the visitors were lodged. They slept on cots beside the beds of the inhabitants, the sickly, the halt, the lame, the mad, the imbecile, the diabetic, those who had weak hearts, those who had cancers in their bodies, those whose eyes were rheumy with trachoma, women with infertile wombs, mothers with deformed children, men threatened with prison or military service, deserters who prayed for a lucky escape, those who had been given up by doctors, those who had been cast out by mankind, those who had been mishandled by earthly justice, the careworn, the yearning, the starving and the satiated, impostors and honest men, all, all, all . . .

Deborah lived with Kluczysk relatives of her husband. She did not sleep. All night she crouched beside Menuchim's basket in the corner, by the stove; darkness was in the room, and darkness in her heart. She no longer dared to call upon God. He seemed to her too lofty, too great, too far away, infinitely far away behind an infinite Heaven. She would have needed a ladder of a million prayers to touch even a hem of God's garment. She sought after the dead who might intercede for her, called upon her parents, upon Menuchim's grandfather, after whom the child had been named, then upon the ancestors of the Jews, Abraham, Isaac, and Jacob, upon the bones of Moses, and, finally, upon Mother Eve herself.

She directed her sighs wherever an advocate might be found. She beat upon a hundred graves, knocked at a hundred doors of Paradise. Fearing that she might not reach the Rabbi the next day because too many petitioners were there, she prayed first for the luck to be there early, as though the healing of her son would then be mere child's play.

At last she saw through the cracks of the black window shutters a few pale strips of daylight. She rose quickly. She lighted the dry pine chips which lay on the hearth, sought and found a teapot, lifted the samovar from the table, threw in the burning chips, shook in charcoal, held the vessel by both handles, tipped it and blew into it, so that the sparks flew out and scorched her face.

She seemed to go through a secret ritual. Soon the water boiled, soon the tea brewed, the family rose, sat down before the earthenware dishes and drank. Then Deborah lifted her son from the basket. He whimpered. She kissed him rapidly many times, with a frantic tenderness; her damp lips resounded upon the grey face, the poor hands, the crooked thighs, the bloated belly of the little one; it was as though she struck the child with her loving motherly mouth. Then she packed him up, tied a cord around the package, and hung her son around her neck, so that her hands would be free. She wanted to clear a way through the mob in front of the door of the Rabbi.

She threw herself into the midst of the waiting crowd with sharp cries. With cruel fists she pushed the weak out of her way; no one could stop her. Whoever, encountering her hand and being pushed aside, looked back at her to repel her was dazzled by the burning pain in her countenance, by her open red mouth out of which a burning breath seemed to stream, by the crystal gleam of the great rolling tears, by the flaming cheeks, by the thick blue veins on her strained throat in which the cries accumulated before they broke forth. Deborah swept along like a torch. With a single harsh cry, which was followed by a gruesome stillness like that of a dead world, Deborah reached the door of the Rabbi and fell before it, the latch in her outstretched right hand. With her left hand she pounded against the brown wood. Menuchim slipped to the ground before her.

Someone opened the door. The Rabbi stood at the window, his back turned to her, a narrow black line. Suddenly he turned to face her. She stopped on the threshold, holding out her son upon both arms, as one offers a sacrifice. She caught a gleam from the man's white countenance, which seemed one with his white beard. She had intended to gaze into the eyes of the Holy One, to convince herself that a powerful goodness really lived in them. But now that she stood there, a sea of tears blurred her vision, and she saw the man behind a white wave of water and salt. He lifted his hand; she thought she recognized two thin fingers, the instrument of blessing. But very near her she heard the voice of the Rabbi although he only whispered:

'Menuchim, Mendel's son, will be healed. There will not be many like him in Israel. Pain will make him wise, ugliness good, bitterness mild, and sickness strong. His eyes will see far and deep. His ears will be clear and full of echoes. His mouth will be silent, but when he opens his lips they will announce good tidings. Have no fear, and go home!'

'When, when, when will he be well?' Deborah whispered.

'After many years,' said the Rabbi, 'but ask me no more. I have no time and this is all I know. Do not leave your son even if he is a great burden to you. Do not send him away from your side; he is yours even as a healthy child is. And now go! . . .'

Outside they cleared a way for her. Her cheeks were pale, her eyes dry, her lips were lightly opened as though she breathed in hope. With grace in her heart she turned homeward.

II

When Deborah returned home, she found her husband at the hearth. Unwillingly he tended the fire, the pot, the wooden spoons. His upright soul was directed upon simple earthly things, and he tolerated no miracles within reach of his eyes. He smiled at his wife's simple faith in the Rabbi. His modest piety required no mediator between God and men.

'Menuchim will be well, but it will take a long time!' With these words Deborah entered the house.

'It will take a long time!' repeated Mendel like an evil echo.

Deborah sighed and again hung the basket from the ceiling. The three older children came in from their play. They fell upon the basket, which they had missed for a few days, and set it to swinging vehemently. Mendel

Singer grabbed his sons, Jonas and Shemariah, with both hands. Miriam, the girl, fled to her mother. Mendel boxed his sons' ears. They howled. He unbuckled his belt and swung it through the air. Mendel Singer felt each smacking blow which struck the backs of his sons as though the leather were the natural continuation of his hand. A dismal tumult broke loose in his head. The warning screams of his wife were drowned unnoticed in his own noise. It was as though one spilled glasses of water into an agitated ocean. He did not know where he stood. He whirled the swinging, cracking belt about, hit the walls, the table, the benches, and did not know which pleased him most, the blows which failed or those which reached their mark.

Finally the clock on the wall struck three, the hour when the pupils assembled in the afternoon. With an empty stomach – for he had eaten nothing – with his throat still choked with excitement, Mendel began to recite the Bible, word for word, verse after verse. The bright choir of children's voices repeated word for word, verse after verse. It was as though the Bible were being tolled by many bells. The torsos of the scholars swung like bells, backward and forward, while over their heads Menuchim's basket swung in almost the same rhythm. Today Mendel's sons participated in the instruction. The father's rage calmed down, cooled, died out, because in the chanting recitative his boys surpassed the others. In order to test them he left the room. The choir of the children sounded on, led by the voices of his sons. He could depend on them.

Jonas, the elder, was strong as a bear. Shemariah, the younger, was sly as a fox. Jonas trotted about, stamping, his head bent forward, his hands hanging, with protuberant cheeks, eternal hunger, and curly hair that grew exuberantly over the edge of his cap. His brother Shemariah followed him, quiet and almost sneaking, with a pointed profile, light, wide-awake eyes, thin arms, hands for ever buried in his pockets. There was never a quarrel between these two. They were too far from each other. Their riches and possessions were kept distinct. They had an agreement. Shemariah made wonderful things out of tin cans, match-boxes, old pots, pieces of horn, and willow twigs. Jonas could have destroyed them with one blast from his strong lungs. But he admired his brother's delicate cleverness. His little black eyes, inquisitive and gay, blinked like sparks above his cheeks.

One day shortly after her return Deborah decided that the time had come to take down Menuchim's basket from the ceiling. Not without solemnity she turned the little one over to the older children. 'You must take him walking!' said Deborah. 'When he gets tired you must carry him. In God's name, don't let him fall! The holy man has said that he will get strong. Do him no harm!' From now on the children's troubles began.

They dragged Menuchim like a misfortune through the town. They let him lie, they let him fall. They ill endured the scorn of their comrades who tagged after them when they took Menuchim walking. The little one had to be carried between his two brothers. He could not put one foot before the other like a human being. His legs shook like two broken hoops, he stopped in his tracks, he collapsed. Finally Jonas and Shemariah let him lie. They stuck him in a corner, half-covered by a sack. There he played with pebbles and with the dung of dogs and horses. He ate everything. He scratched the lime from the walls and stuffed his mouth full of it, then coughed until he was blue in the face. He lay in the corner like a scrap of rubbish.

Sometimes he would start to cry. Then the boys would send Miriam to him to comfort him. Dainty, coquettish, with thin hopping legs, ugly hate and disgust in her heart, she would approach her ridiculous brother. The delicacy with which she stroked his distorted ash-grey countenance had something murderous in it. She would look about carefully, right and left, and then pinch her brother in the thigh. He would yell and neighbours would look out of the windows. She pulled down her mouth in an expression of grief. Everybody had pity on her and asked her what was the matter.

One rainy summer day the children dragged Menuchim out of the house and stuck him in a vat, in which rainwater had collected for half a year. Maggots swam about in it, decayed fruit and mouldy bread crusts. They held him by his crooked legs and pushed his broad grey head a dozen times into the water. Then, with pounding hearts and glowing cheeks, they pulled him out in the joyful and gruesome expectation that they were holding a corpse. But Menuchim lived. He rattled in his throat, spat up the water, the maggots, the

19

mouldy bread, the fruit rinds, and lived. Nothing happened to him. Silent and anxious, the children then carried him home. They thought they had seen God's finger shaken at them and the two boys and the girl were gripped by fear. For a whole day they said nothing to each other. Their tongues clove to the roofs of their mouths; their lips opened to form a word, but no sound issued from their throats. The rain stopped, the sun shone, the little brooks flowed gaily along the edges of the streets. It was time to launch paper ships and watch them sail towards the canal. But nothing happened. The children crept back into the house like dogs. All afternoon they waited for the death of Menuchim, but Menuchim did not die.

Menuchim did not die; he lived, a mighty cripple. From now on, Deborah's womb was dry and barren. Menuchim was the last deformed fruit of her body. It was as though her womb refused to bring forth more misfortune. In hasty moments she embraced her husband. The moments were short as lightning, dry lightning on a distant summer horizon. Long, cruel, and sleepless were Deborah's nights. A wall of cold glass separated her from her husband. Her breasts withered; her body swelled, as if in mockery of her barrenness; her thighs became heavy, and lead hung to her feet.

One morning in summer she awakened earlier than Mendel. A chirping sparrow at the window had disturbed her. His pipings were still in her ears, recalling something dreamed, something happy, like the voice of a ray of sunshine. The early dawn pushed in through the holes and cracks of the wooden window shutters, and, although the edges of the furniture were still blurred in the shadows of the night, Deborah's eyes were already clear, her thoughts hard, her heart cool. She cast a glance upon the sleeping man and discovered the first white hairs in his black beard. He cleared his throat in his sleep. He snored.

Quickly she sprang before the blurred mirror. She combed through her thin hair with cold fingers, drew one strand after another over her forehead, and looked for white hairs. She thought she found a single one, grasped it with the hard tongs of two fingers, and tore it out. Then she opened her chemise before the mirror. She saw her flaccid breasts, lifted them, let them fall. stroked her hand over her empty yet swollen body, saw the blue branching veins on her thighs, and decided to go to bed again.

She turned, and her scared glance met the opened eye of her husband. 'What are you looking at?' she cried. He did not answer. It was as though the open eye did not belong to him, as though he himself still slept. It had opened independently of him. It had become independently inquisitive. The white of the eye seemed whiter than usual. The pupil was tiny. The eye reminded Deborah of a frozen lake with a black spot in it. It could hardly have been open a minute but to Deborah this minute seemed a decade.

Mendel's eye closed again. He breathed quietly on. He was undoubtedly asleep. Outside, a distant trill from a million larks arose, above the house and under the sky. The dawning heat of the young day began to penetrate into the darkened room. Soon the clock would strike six, the hour when Mendel Singer was accustomed to rise. Deborah did not move. She remained where she had stood when she turned again towards the bed, with the mirror at her back. Never before had she stood thus, listening, without purpose, with no need, without curiosity, without desire. She was waiting for nothing. Yet it seemed to her that she was expecting something very special. All her senses were awake in her as never before, and a few new unknown senses were awake in support of the familiar ones. She saw, heard, felt, a thousandfold.

And nothing happened. Only a summer morning dawned, only larks trilled in the distance, only sun rays forced themselves warmly through the cracks in the shutters, and the broad shadows on the edges of the furniture grew smaller and smaller, and the clock ticked and struck six, and the man breathed. The children lay in the corner, close to the hearth, without a sound, visible to Deborah but far away, as though in another room. Nothing happened. And yet it seemed as though everything must happen.

The clock struck like a release. Mendel Singer awoke, sat straight up in bed and stared in astonishment at his wife. 'Why aren't you in bed?' he asked, and rubbed his eyes. He coughed and spat. Nothing in his words and nothing in his mien betrayed that his left eye had been open and had gazed independently. Perhaps he had forgotten; perhaps Deborah had been mistaken.

From this day on all desire between Mendel Singer and his wife ceased. Like two people of the same sex they went to sleep, slept through the night, awoke in the morning. They became shy with each other and were silent, as in the first days of their marriage. At the beginning of their desire there had been shame, and at the end of their desire there was shame.

Then it also was overcome. They spoke to each other again. Their eyes no longer avoided each other, and their faces and bodies aged in the same rhythm, like the faces and bodies of twins.

The summer was sultry and poor in rain. Doors and windows stood open. The children were seldom at home. Outside they grew quickly, vitalized by the sun.

Even Menuchim grew. His legs, to be sure, remained crooked, but unquestionably they became longer. So did the rest of his body. Suddenly, one morning, he let out a strange, shrill cry. Then he was silent. A little while later he said quite clearly and understandably: 'Mama.'

Deborah threw herself upon him, and from her eyes, which had long remained dry, tears flowed, hot, strong, big, salty, painful, and sweet. 'Say Mama!'

'Mama,' echoed the little one.

A dozen times he repeated the word. A hundred times Deborah repeated it. Not in vain had been her prayers. Menuchim spoke. And this one word of the deformed child was sublime as a revelation, mighty as thunder, warm as love, gracious as Heaven, wide as the earth, fertile as a field, sweet as a sweet fruit. It was more than the health of the healthy children. It meant that

Menuchim would be strong and big, wise and good, as the words of the blessing had promised.

To be sure no other understandable sounds issued from Menuchim's throat. For a long time this one word, which he had brought out after such a terrible silence, meant food and drink, sleep and love, pleasure and pain, heaven and earth. Although he used this word for every situation, he seemed to his mother as loquacious as a preacher and as rich in expression as a poet. She understood all the words which were buried in this single one. She neglected the older children. She turned away from them. She had but one son, an only son: Menuchim.

III

PERHAPS BLESSINGS NEED a longer time for their fulfilment than curses. Ten years had passed since Menuchim had spoken his first and only word. He could still say nothing else.

Sometimes when Deborah is alone in the house with her sick son, she bolts the door, sits down beside Menuchim on the floor, and stares into the little one's face. Then she remembers the dreadful day in summer when the Countess drove before the church. She sees the open door of the church. A golden gleam from a thousand candles, from coloured pictures wreathed in light, from three priests in robes who stand far back near the altar, with black beards and white, hovering hands, shines out into the sunny, dusty square. Deborah is in the third month; Menuchim stirs in her body; she holds delicate little Miriam fast by the hand. Suddenly there is shouting. It drowns out the chant of the prayerful in the church. There is heard the clacking trample of horses; a cloud of dust whirls up; the dark-blue equipage of the Countess stops before the church. The peasant children hurrah. The beggars on the steps hobble towards the carriage to kiss the hand of the Countess. Suddenly Miriam breaks loose. In no time she has disappeared. Deborah trembles; she freezes, in the midst of the heat. Where is Miriam? she asks one peasant child after another. The Countess descends. Deborah approaches the carriage. The coachman with the silver buttons on his dark-blue livery sits so high that he can overlook everything. 'Did you see where the little black-haired girl ran to?' asks Deborah, her head stretched backward, her eyes blinded by the sun and by the coachman's bright buttons. The coachman points with his white-gloved left hand towards the church. Miriam had gone in there.

Deborah considers a moment, then dashes into the church, into the midst of the golden shining, the full-voiced music, the organ's roar. In the entrance stands Miriam. Deborah grabs the child, drags her towards the square, rushes down the hot, white steps, flees as before a conflagration. She wants to beat the child but she is afraid.

She runs, dragging the child behind her, into a narrow street. Now she is quieter. 'Tell your father nothing of this,' she pants. 'Do you hear, Miriam?'

From this day on, Deborah knew that a misfortune

was under way. She carried a misfortune in her womb. She knew it and was silent.

Now she pushes the bolt back, there is a knock on the door. Mendel is home.

His beard is prematurely grey. Prematurely withered were also the face, the body, and the hands of Deborah. Strong and slow as a bear was the oldest son, Jonas; sly and nimble as a fox was the younger son, Shemariah; thoughtless and coquettish as a gazelle, the sister Miriam.

When Miriam hurried through the streets on errands, slender and small, a shimmering shadow, a brown face, a wide red mouth, a golden-yellow shawl knotted in two flying wings under her chin, and with two old eyes in the midst of the brown youth of her countenance, she attracted the attention of the officers of the garrison, and remained in their careless, pleasure-seeking minds. Occasionally one would lie in wait for her. She noticed nothing about her pursuers except the impression they made upon her outer senses: a silver clinking and rustling of spurs and arms, a pervasive smell of pomade and shaving soap, a fulminating gleam of gold buttons, silver braid, and bright-red reins of Russia leather. It was little, it was enough. Just behind the outer portal of her senses curiosity lurked in Miriam, curiosity which is the sister of youth and the awakener of desire. The girl fled before her pursuers in sweet and hot anxiety, only, in order to drag out the painfully exciting pleasure, she fled through many by-ways, prolonging her flight many minutes. She fled in a roundabout fashion. Only, in

27

order to flee again, Miriam would leave home oftener than was necessary. At the street corner she would stop and cast a glance backward, baiting her huntsmen. It was Miriam's only pleasure. Even if there had been anyone at hand who could understand her, she would have kept her mouth closed. For delights are stronger the longer they remain secret.

Miriam did not yet know how threatening would be her relationship to the strange and terrible world of the military and how heavy were the destinies which had begun to collect over the heads of Mendel Singer, his wife, and his children. For Jonas and Shemariah were already at the age when, according to the law, they should become soldiers and, according to the tradition of their fathers, they must rescue themselves from military service.

A gracious and provident God had bestowed upon other youngsters some physical disability which caused them little inconvenience and protected them from this evil. Some had only one eye, some limped, this one had a rupture, that one twitched uncontrollably with his arms and legs, a few had weak lungs, others weak hearts, one heard badly and another stuttered and a third just suffered from general debility.

But it seemed as though in the family of Mendel Singer little Menuchim had taken upon himself the whole catalogue of human suffering which a kind nature might otherwise have divided among all the members. Mendel's older sons were healthy. No defect could be found on their bodies, and they had to begin to torture themselves, to fast and drink black coffee and to hope for at least some temporary heart disease, although the war against Japan was already over.

And so their troubles began. They ate nothing, they did not sleep, they reeled about, weak and trembling, day and night. Their eyes were reddened and swollen, their necks thin and their heads heavy.

Deborah loved them again. In order to pray for her older sons, she again made a pilgrimage to the cemetery. As once she had prayed for health for Menuchim so now she petitioned for an illness for Jonas and Shemariah. The military arose before her anxious eyes like a great mountain of slippery ice, like a huge, clanking instrument of torture. She saw corpses, nothing but corpses. High and shining, his spurred feet in red blood, sat the Tsar awaiting the sacrifice of her sons.

Manoeuvres had begun! This alone was for her the greatest of shocks. She did not dare even to think about a new war. She scorned her husband. Mendel Singer, what was he? A teacher, a stupid teacher of stupid children. She had had something else in mind when she was still a young girl.

Meanwhile, Mendel Singer was no less burdened with cares than his wife. On the Sabbath, in the synagogue, when the legally prescribed prayer for the Tsar had to be made, Mendel thought about his sons and what they were facing. Already he saw them in the hateful denim uniforms of fresh recruits. They ate pork and were beaten by officers with riding whips. They carried guns and bayonets. Often he sighed unconsciously in the midst of his prayers, in the midst of giving instruction, in the midst of a silence. Even strangers regarded him anxiously. No one had ever asked after his sick child, but everyone inquired about his healthy sons.

Finally, on the twenty-sixth of March, both brothers journeyed to Targi. Both drew service numbers in the lots. Both were perfectly healthy. Both were accepted. They were allowed to pass one more summer at home. They had to report in the autumn. On a Wednesday they became soldiers; on a Sunday they returned home.

On a Sunday they returned home, equipped with free railway passes from the State. Already they travelled at the expense of the Tsar. Many of their kind travelled with them. It was a slow train. They sat on wooden benches among peasants. The peasants sang and were drunk. They all smoked black tobacco, with the smoke of which a distant reminder of sweat was blended. They told each other stories. Jonas and Shemariah did not separate for a minute. It was almost their first journey on the railway. Often they changed seats with each other. Each of them wished to sit for a few minutes at the window and look at the landscape. In Jonas's eyes it was flat; it bored him. The train glided smoothly over the flat land, like a sleigh over snow. The fields were framed in the windows, the peasant women in their coloured shawls waved. Wherever a group of them appeared, the peasants in the train greeted them with a roar.

Dark, shy, and anxious, the two Jews sat amongst the peasants, pushed into a corner by the exuberance of the drunken men.

'I should like to be a peasant,' Jonas suddenly said.

'Not I,' answered Shemariah.

'But I would really like to be a peasant,' repeated Jonas. 'I'd like to get drunk and sleep with the girls.'

'I want to be what I am,' said Shemariah. 'A Jew like my father, Mendel Singer. No soldier, and sober.'

'I'm sort of glad I'm going to be a soldier,' said Jonas.

'You'll have a nice time of it! I'd rather be a rich man and see life.'

'What's life?'

'Life,' declared Shemariah, 'is in the big towns. The trams run in the middle of the streets, all the stores are as big as our gendarmerie barracks, and the show windows are even bigger. I've seen picture postcards. You don't need any door to go into the shops. The windows reach to the ground.'

'Hey, why are you so down in the mouth?' a peasant suddenly called at them from the opposite corner.

Jonas and Shemariah acted as though they had not heard or as though the question was not for them. To pretend to be deaf when a peasant spoke to them was in their blood. For a thousand years nothing good had ever come of it when a peasant asked a question and a Jew replied.

'Hey!' said the peasant and got up.

Jonas and Shemariah also got up.

'Yes, I spoke to you Jews,' said the peasant. 'Have you had anything to drink yet?'

'Had our drink,' said Shemariah.

'I haven't,' said Jonas.

31

The peasant brought out a bottle which he had worn on his breast under his tunic. It was warm and slippery and stank more of the peasant than of its contents. Jonas put it to his mouth. He revealed full, deep-red lips. One saw his strong white teeth on either side of the neck of the brown bottle. Jonas drank and drank. He did not notice the light hand of his brother which pulled his sleeve warningly. Like an enormous infant he held the bottle in both hands. His shirt shimmered white through the worn thin stuff on his crooked elbow. Regularly, like a piston in a machine, his Adam's apple rose and fell under the skin of his neck. A soft choking gurgle sounded in his throat. Everybody watched how the Jew drank.

Jonas was finished. The empty bottle fell out of his hand into his brother Shemariah's lap. He himself followed it as though he had to take the same path. The peasant stretched out his hand and dumbly asked Shemariah for the bottle. Then he caressed the broad shoulders of the sleeping Jonas with the tip of his boot.

They reached Podvorsk where they had to change. It was still seven versts to Yurki, where they had to go on foot. Who knew whether anyone would give them a lift on their way! All the travellers helped heave Jonas upright. As soon as he got outside he was sober again.

They walked on. It was night. They felt the moon was there behind milky clouds. A few irregular spots of earth darkened the snowy fields like the mouths of craters. Spring seemed to be wafted out of the woods.

Jonas and Shemariah walked quickly on the narrow

path. They heard the sharp crackle of the brittle snow under their boots. They carried their round white bundles over their shoulders on sticks. Once or twice Shemariah tried to start a conversation with his brother. Jonas did not answer. He was ashamed because he had drunk and collapsed like any peasant.

In the places where the path was so narrow that both brothers could not walk side by side, Jonas let the younger lead the way. He would have preferred Shemariah to walk in front of him all the way. Where the path became broader, he slowed his step in the hope that Shemariah would go ahead without waiting for him. But it was as though the younger boy feared to lose the elder. Since he had seen that Jonas could get drunk, he no longer trusted him. He doubted the common sense of the older boy. He felt himself responsible for him.

Jonas knew what his brother was thinking. A vast insane scorn boiled in his heart. 'Shemariah is ridiculous,' thought Jonas. 'He's as thin as a ghost, he can't even hold his stick, he keeps shifting it about, the bundle will fall in the dirt yet.' At the picture of Shemariah's white bundle slipping from the smooth stick into the black dirt of the road, Jonas laughed aloud.

'What are you laughing at?' asked Shemariah.

'At you!' answered Jonas.

'I have a better right to laugh at you,' said Shemariah.

Again they were silent. The pine forest grew black around them. The silence seemed to come not out of themselves but out of it. From time to time a stray wind rose, a homeless wind. A willow bush moved in its sleep, twigs rubbed dryly against each other, clouds fled swiftly over the sky.

'Well, we are soldiers now!' said Shemariah suddenly.

'Sure,' said Jonas. 'And what were we before? We haven't any trade. Should we become teachers like our father?'

'Better than to be soldiers,' said Shemariah. 'I might be a merchant and go out into the world!'

'Soldiers are also part of the world, and I could never be a merchant,' said Jonas.

'You're drunk!'

'I'm as sober as you are. I can drink and still be sober. I can be a soldier and see the world. I'd like to be a peasant. I tell you that – and I'm not drunk . . .'

Shemariah shrugged his shoulders. They walked farther. Towards morning they heard the cocks crowing in distant barnyards. 'That must be Yurki,' said Shemariah.

'No, it's Bytók!' said Jonas.

'Call it Bytók,' said Shemariah.

A cart clattered and rattled around the next turn of the road. The day was cloudy as the night had been. No difference between moon and sun. Snow began to fall. Soft falling snow. Ravens started up, cawing.

'Look at the birds,' said Shemariah, only as an excuse to make up with his brother.

'They're ravens, that's what they are!' said Jonas. 'Birds!' he mocked his brother scornfully.

'All right!' said Shemariah. 'Ravens!'

It was really Bytók. An hour later they came to Yurki. Three hours more and they would be home.

The snow became thicker and softer as the day wore on, as though it fell from the hidden sun. In a few minutes the whole country was white, even the isolated willows along the way, and the scattered groups of birches among the fields, white, white, white. Only the two young Jews, striding along, were black. The snow also fell on them but it seemed to melt more quickly on their backs. Their long black coats flapped. The skirts struck with a hard regular beat against the shafts of their high leather boots, and the thicker it snowed, the faster they walked. Peasants who passed them walked slowly, with bent knees. They were white; on their broad shoulders lay the snow as upon thick boughs, at once heavy and light. At peace with the snow they walked about in it as in a home. Sometimes they stopped and looked back after the two black men as if they were unusual apparitions, although the sight of Jews was not strange to them.

The brothers arrived home out of breath. Twilight had already begun. From afar they heard the sing-song of the studying children. It was wafted towards them like a mother's voice, like a father's words; it carried their whole childhood out towards them. It meant and contained everything that they had seen, comprehended, smelled, and felt since the hour of their birth: the sing-song of the studying children. It contained the aroma of hot and spicy dishes, the black and white shimmer of their father's face and beard, the echo of their mother's sigh, the whimpers of Menuchim, Mendel Singer's whispered evening prayers, millions of indescribable common and special experiences. Both brothers reacted in the same way to the melody which floated towards them through the snow as they neared their father's house. Their hearts beat in the same rhythm. The door flew open at their approach; their mother, Deborah, had watched them coming through the window.

'We have been taken,' said Jonas, without any other greeting.

A dreadful silence suddenly filled the room in which a moment before the voices of the children had sounded, an infinite silence much vaster than the space which contained it, and nevertheless born out of the one little word 'taken' that Jonas had just spoken. In the middle of a word that they had memorized, the children stopped their lesson. Mendel who had been walking up and down in the room stopped in his tracks, stared before him, lifted his arms and let them fall. The mother, Deborah, sank upon one of the two stools which always stood near the stove as though she had long been waiting to take up the role of a mourning mother. Miriam, the daughter, groped her way to the corner; her heart beat loudly; she thought that everyone must hear it. The children sat as though nailed to their places. Their legs in gaily striped woollen stockings, which had swung continually through the lesson, hung lifeless under the table. Outside, it snowed uninterruptedly, and the soft white of the flakes sent a dull stream of light through the window into the room and upon the faces of the silent people. Sometimes one heard an ember crackle in the stove, and the gentle rattle of the doorposts as the wind shook them. With their sticks still over their shoulders, the white bundles still on the sticks, the brothers stood in the doorway, heralds of misfortune and misfortune's children.

Suddenly Deborah cried: 'Mendel, run, go and ask people for advice!'

Mendel Singer stroked his beard. The silence was broken, the children's legs began to swing, the brothers dropped their bundles and sticks and approached the table.

'What nonsense are you talking?' said Mendel Singer. 'Where shall I go? And whom shall I ask for advice? Who will help a poor teacher and how can anyone help me? What sort of help do you await from mankind when God has so punished us?'

Deborah did not answer. She sat still for a little while upon the stool. Then she arose; kicked the stool as though it had been a dog, so that it spun away with a great din; grabbed her brown shawl, which had been lying on the floor like a little hill of wool; bound up her head and throat; tied the fringes in a hard knot at the nape of her neck with a furious gesture as though she wanted to strangle herself; became red in the face; stood there hissing as though she were filled with boiling water, and suddenly spat. She fired the white spittle like a poison shot before Mendel Singer's feet. And as though with this gesture alone she had not sufficiently expressed her contempt, she sent a cry after the spittle, which sounded very like a *pfui!*, but which could not be clearly understood. Before the astonished onlookers had really comprehended, she threw open the door. A strong wind scattered white flakes into the room, blew into Mendel Singer's face, grasped the children by their hanging legs. Then the door banged shut. Deborah had gone.

She ran aimlessly through the little streets, holding the middle of the way; like a dark-brown colossus she rushed through the white snow until she sank in it. She stumbled over her clothes, fell, scrambled up with astonishing nimbleness, ran farther – still she did not know whither; it was as though her feet knew a goal that her mind was unconscious of. Twilight fell faster than the snowflakes, the first yellow lights glimmered, the few people who came out of the houses to close their shutters turned their heads to look after Deborah and stood staring at her although they were freezing.

Deborah ran in the direction of the cemetery. As she reached the little wooden gate she fell again. She pulled herself up, the gate would not give way, the snow had jammed it shut. Deborah heaved her shoulder against it. Now she was inside. The wind howled over the graves. Today the dead seemed more dead than ever. Out of the twilight the night deepened fast, black, black, and shot through with the gleam of snow. Deborah sank down before one of the first gravestones in the first row. With numbed fists she freed it from snow, as though she wanted to assure herself that her voice would penetrate more easily if this smothering layer between her prayer and the ear of the blessed were cleared away. And then a cry burst forth from Deborah. It sounded as though it came from a trumpet in which a human heart had been imprisoned. People heard this cry throughout the village, but they forgot it immediately. For the stillness which followed it was not heard. From time to time Deborah whimpered lightly, a gentle motherly whimper which the night swallowed, the snow buried, and only the dead heard.

IV

NOT FAR FROM the Kluczysk relatives of Mendel Singer
lived Kapturak, a man of no particular age, without a family, without friends, brisk and busy, and in
right with the authorities. Deborah set about to obtain
his help. Of the seventy roubles which Kapturak
demanded before he would even discuss things with
his clients, she had a bare twenty-five, saved secretly
during the long years of toil and laid away in a durable
leather bag under a floor-board in a place which she
alone knew. Every Friday she took it up stealthily when
she scoured the floor. To her maternal faith the difference of forty-five roubles seemed smaller than the sum
which she already possessed. For to the latter she added
the years in which she had piled up her money, the sac-
rifices to which every half-rouble owed its existence,

and the many quiet, warm joys she had felt in counting it.

Mendel Singer sought in vain to describe to her the inaccessibility of Kapturak, his hard heart, and his greedy pocket. 'What are you thinking of, Deborah?' said Mendel Singer. 'The poor are powerless, God does not throw them golden stones from Heaven, they never win in the lottery, and they have to bear their fate with humility. To one He gives and from the other He takes away. I do not know why He punishes us, first with the illness of Menuchim, and now with the health of the other children. Ah, the poor man has it hard; when he has sinned and when he is ill, he has it hard. Let each suffer his lot! Let the sons serve, they won't go to the bad; against the will of Heaven there is no power. "He is the thunder and the lightning, He arches Himself over the whole world, no man can escape Him," thus is it written.'

But Deborah answered with her hands braced against her hips above the bundle of rusty keys: 'God helps those who help themselves. That's also written, Mendel! You always know the false verses by heart. Thousands of verses are written, but you notice all of the unnecessary ones! You've become silly from teaching children! You give them what little sense you have, and they give you all their stupidity. You're a teacher, Mendel, a teacher!'

Mendel Singer was not vain either of his wits or of his profession. But the taunts of Deborah ate into him; her reproaches slowly broke down his good nature; and in his heart the white flames of indignation were already kindling. He turned away in order no longer to see his wife's face. It was as though he had already known it such a long time, far longer than the time since their wedding, perhaps since his childhood. For many years it had looked to him exactly as on the day of his marriage. He had not seen how the flesh had withered on the cheeks like prettily painted plaster dropping from a wall, how the skin stretched itself across the nose, in order to flap the more loosely under the chin, how the eyelids wrinkled into a network above the eyes, and how the blackness of the eyes themselves faded to a cool and sober brown, cool, sensible, and hopeless.

One day – he did not remember when it could have been (perhaps it was that very morning when he himself had slept and only his eye had surprised Deborah before the mirror) – one day, anyhow, recognition had dawned on him. It was like a second marriage, this time with the ugliness, the bitterness, the advancing age of his wife. He found her closer to him than ever, almost physically joined to him, inseparable and for Eternity, but unendurable, painful, and even a little hateful. From a woman with whom he had only coupled himself in the darkness, she had become a disease that was bound to him by day and by night, belonging entirely to him, no longer something he shared with all the world, whose faithful enmity was to mean his own destruction. Of course he was only a teacher! So had his father been and his grandfather before him. He himself could not be otherwise. Thus one attacked his very existence when one criticized his profession, one sought to erase him from the lists of the living. And against this Mendel Singer defended himself.

Actually he was glad that Deborah was going away. Already, now, while she was making preparations for the journey, the house was empty. Jonas and Shemariah walked about the streets; Miriam sat with neighbours or went for walks. At home, around midday, before the scholars returned, Mendel and Menuchim remained alone. Mendel ate a barley soup which he had cooked for himself, and in his earthenware plate left a bit over for Menuchim. He slid the bolt, that the child should not creep through the door as he liked to do. Then the father went into a corner, lifted the child upon his knee, and began to feed it.

He loved these quiet hours. He was glad to be alone with his son. Yes, he sometimes wondered if it would not be better if they stayed alone altogether, without the mother, without the brothers and sister. After Menuchim had swallowed the soup, spoonful after spoonful, his father would set him upon the table, sit still before him, and stare with tender curiosity into the broad sallow face with its wrinkled brow, netted eyelids, and flaccid double chin. He tried to guess what might be going on in that broad skull, to gaze in through the eyes as through a window in the brain, and by talking to him, sometimes loudly, sometimes softly, to draw from the stolid boy some sort of sign. He would repeat Menuchim's name ten times, moving his lips slowly so that the boy could see him say it if he could not hear. But Menuchim never responded.

Then Mendel would take a spoon, strike it against a tea glass, and immediately Menuchim would turn his head, and a tiny light would flame in his great, grey, liquid eyes. Mendel would ring again, begin to sing a little song and to beat time on the glass with the spoon, and Menuchim would clearly display uneasiness, turn his great head with a certain effort, and dangle his legs. 'Mama, Mama!' he would cry out all the while.

Mendel stood up, fetched the great black Bible, held the first page open before Menuchim's face, and intoned, in the chant in which he was accustomed to instruct his pupils, the first verse: 'In the beginning God created the heaven and the earth.' He waited a moment in the hope that Menuchim would repeat the words, but Menuchim did not move. Only in his eyes the listening light still stood. Then Mendel laid the book away, gazed sadly at his son, and chanted in his monotonous sing-song:

'Listen to me, Menuchim, I am all alone! Your brothers have grown big and strange, they go to the army. Your mother is a woman, what can I expect of her? You are my youngest son, my last and most recent hopes are all planted in you. Why do you remain silent, Menuchim? You are truly my son! Look, Menuchim, and repeat after me the words: "In the beginning God created the heaven and the earth . . ."'

Mendel waited another moment. Menuchim did not move. Then Mendel rang again with the spoon on the glass. Menuchim turned around, and Mendel, catching as though with both hands at this moment of wakefulness, sang again: 'Hear me, Menuchim! I am old, you alone are left of all my children! Listen to me, and say after me: "In the beginning God created the heaven and the earth . . ." '

But Menuchim did not move.

Then with a heavy sigh Mendel set Menuchim again upon the floor. He slid back the bolt and stepped before the door to wait for his scholars. Menuchim crept after him and squatted on the doorsill. The tower clock struck seven notes, four deep ones and three high ones. Then Menuchim cried: 'Mama, Mama!' And as Mendel turned towards him, he saw that the little one stretched his head in the air as though he breathed in the music of the bells.

'Why am I so afflicted?' thought Mendel, and he explored his conscience for sins but found none that was grave.

The scholars came. He re-entered the house with them and, while he walked up and down through the room, he admonished this one or that, rapped one on the fingers, nudged another lightly in the ribs, and all the time he was thinking: What sin did I commit? What sin did I commit?

Meanwhile, Deborah went to the driver Sameshkin and asked him whether he would take her to Kluczysk sometime in the next few days for nothing.

'Yes,' said the driver Sameshkin. He sat on the bare bench around the stove, without moving, his feet in great yellow bags tied round with string, and he stank of home-brewed spirits.

Deborah smelled out the brandy as though it were

an enemy. It was the dangerous smell of the peasants, the forerunner of incomprehensible passions, the accompaniment of pogroms.

'Yes,' said Sameshkin, 'if the roads were better!'

'You took me once in the autumn, when the roads were still worse.'

'You're wrong. It was a dry summer day.'

'Not at all,' answered Deborah, 'it was autumn, and it rained, and I went to the Rabbi.'

'You see,' said Sameshkin, and his two feet in their rags began to swing softly, because the bench was rather high, and Sameshkin was rather short. 'You see,' he said, 'that time when you went to the Rabbi was just before your Jewish holidays, and so I took you with me. But this time you aren't going to the Rabbi!'

'I am going on important business,' said Deborah. 'Jonas and Shemariah will never be soldiers!'

'I was a soldier, too,' Sameshkin commented. 'Seven years, though I sat in prison for two of them because I stole. That's nothing!'

Deborah became desperate. All his talk only showed her how foreign he was to her, to her and to her sons, who did not steal and who would never go to jail. She determined to drive her bargain quickly. 'How much must I pay you?'

'Nothing at all. I'm not looking for money. I just don't want to go! The white horse is old, the brown one has lost two shoes. And he eats oats the whole day long, when he's run only two versts. I can't keep him any longer, I'm going to sell him. Anyhow, being a driver is no life!'

'Jonas will drive the brown horse to the blacksmith,' said Deborah insistently. 'He will pay for the shoeing himself.'

'Maybe,' answered Sameshkin. 'If Jonas wants to do that himself he'll have to have a new wheel made, too.'

'That, too,' promised Deborah. 'So then, we can start next week!'

Thus she journeyed to Kluczysk, to the uncanny Kapturak. Of course she would much rather have gone to the Rabbi, for certainly one word from his thin, holy lips would have been more valuable than the patronage of Kapturak. But the Rabbi received no one between Passover and Pentecost, except in the most urgent cases, where it was a matter of life and death. She met Kapturak in the taproom, where he sat in a corner, at the window, surrounded by peasants and Jews, writing. His cap, with the lining turned upwards, lay on the table, next to the papers, like an outstretched hand, and many silver pieces rested in it already, and drew the eyes of all those who stood around him. From time to time, Kapturak counted them, although he knew that no one would dare to take even a kopek. He wrote petitions, love letters, and postal checks for the illiterate. (He could also cut hair and extract teeth.)

'I have a very important matter to discuss with you,' said Deborah, talking over the heads of the bystanders.

Kapturak shoved back all the papers with a single gesture. The people scattered. He reached for his cap, shook out the money into his hollowed hand, and tied it up in a handkerchief. Then he invited Deborah to sit down.

She looked into his hard little eyes, which were like light, staring buttons of horn. 'My sons have been conscripted,' she said.

'You are a poor woman,' said Kapturak, in an absent, singing voice, as though he were reading a fortune from cards. 'You have not been able to save any money, and no one can help you.'

'But I have saved.'

'How much?'

'Twenty-four roubles and seventy kopeks. But I've spent one rouble of that already, in order to get here to see you.'

'So you've got twenty-three roubles left?'

'Twenty-three roubles and seventy kopeks.'

Kapturak lifted his right hand, the index and middle fingers spread apart. 'And two sons?'

'Yes,' whispered Deborah.

'But a single one costs twenty-five roubles!'

'For me, too?'

'For you, too!'

For half an hour she bargained. At the end of it, Kapturak was satisfied with twenty-three roubles – for one. 'At least one of them!' thought Deborah.

But under way, while she sat on Sameshkin's wagon, and the wheels rattled in her insides, and in her head, the situation seemed to her more miserable than ever. Who could choose between her two sons? Jonas or

Shemariah? She asked herself this question tirelessly. Better one than both, said her reason, while her heart complained.

When she came home and began to report Kapturak's judgment to her sons, Jonas, the older, interrupted her to say: 'I'm willing to join up.'

Deborah, the daughter Miriam, Shemariah, and Mendel Singer waited as though turned to wood. Finally, when Jonas said nothing more, Shemariah spoke:

'That's a brother! You're a good brother!'

'No,' said Jonas. 'I'd like to be a soldier.'

'Perhaps they will let you off in half a year,' his father comforted him.

'No,' answered Jonas. 'I don't want to get off. I'll stay with the soldiers.'

All murmured the evening prayer. Silently they undressed. Then Miriam, in her chemise, walked coquettishly on her toes to the lamp, and blew it out. They went to sleep.

The next day, Jonas had disappeared. They looked for him all morning. Finally, late in the evening, Miriam caught sight of him. He was riding a white horse, wore a brown blouse, and a soldier's cap.

'Are you a soldier already?' cried Miriam.

'Not yet,' said Jonas, and stopped the horse. 'Give my love to Father and Mother. I've got a job with Sameshkin, for the time being, until I join up. Tell them that I couldn't stand it at home any longer, though I like you all.'

With this, he let his willow switch whistle, pulled on the reins, and rode on.

From now on, he was Sameshkin's stable boy. He currycombed the white horse and the brown, slept beside them in the stall, breathed in enjoyably the acrid smell of urine and sour sweat through distended nostrils. He got their oats and pails of water, hung new bells on the harnesses, filled the troughs, changed the dirty hay in the two wagons for clean straw, drank *samogonka* with Sameshkin, got drunk, and got the girls in a family way.

At home they mourned him as one lost, but they did not forget him. The summer came, hot and dry. The evenings sank late and golden over the land. Before Sameshkin's hut, Jonas sat and played the accordion. He was very drunk, and did not recognize his own father, who sometimes slunk by, a shadow afraid of itself, a father who never ceased to wonder that this, his son, had sprung from his own loins.

V

O<small>N THE TWENTIETH</small> of August a messenger appeared at
Mendel Singer's house, to fetch Shemariah. They
had been expecting Kapturak's messenger any day. Yet
when he stood before them in the flesh, they were surprised and shocked. He was an ordinary man, of
ordinary height and ordinary appearance, with a blue
soldier's cap on his head, and a thin, twisted cigarette in
his mouth. When they invited him to come in, sit down,
and drink a glass of tea, he declined.

'I'd rather wait outside,' he said, in a tone which indi-
cated that he was accustomed to waiting outside.

But the man's decision set the family of Mendel
Singer into even more feverish excitement. Time and
again they saw the blue-capped man appear like a guard

before the window, and each time their movements became more active. They packed Shemariah's things, a suit of clothes, prayer rolls, provisions for the journey, a bread knife. Miriam collected the things; she brought more and more together. Menuchim, whose head already reached to the top of the table, stretched up his chin, stupid and inquisitive, and continually babbled the one word that he knew: Mama!

Mendel Singer stood at the window and drummed against the pane. Deborah wept silently, one tear after another rolled from her eyes to her distorted mouth. When Shemariah's bundle was ready, it seemed to them all too poverty-stricken, and with helpless eyes they searched the room in the hope of discovering some little thing which they could add to it. Until this moment they had not spoken to each other. Now, when the white bundle lay beside its stick on the table, Mendel Singer turned away from the window, towards the room, and said to his son: 'Don't forget to send us word as soon as you possibly can!'

Now Deborah sobbed aloud, stretched out her arms, and embraced her son. They clung to each other long. Then Shemariah tore himself loose, walked to his sister, and kissed her resoundingly on both cheeks. His father spread his hands above the son, in a blessing, and hastily murmured something unintelligible. Then Shemariah timidly approached the goggling Menuchim. For the first time it was necessary to embrace the sick child, and it seemed to Shemariah that it was not a brother whom he must kiss, but a symbol that could give no answer.

Everyone wanted to say something more. But no one found a word. They knew that this was a final farewell. In the best case, Shemariah would escape abroad, hale and healthy. In the worst, he could be caught on the border, then court-martialled, or shot by the border guard, then and there. What is there for people to say to each other, when they part for life?

Shemariah shouldered his bundle, and pushed the door open with his foot. He did not look back again. He tried, in that moment in which he stepped over the threshold, to forget the house and all of its inhabitants. Behind his back one more shrill cry sounded from Deborah's throat. The door closed. With the feeling that his mother had in the same moment swooned, Shemariah approached his guide.

'Right back of the market-place,' said the man with the blue cap. 'The horses are waiting there.'

As they passed Sameshkin's hut, Shemariah stopped. He cast a glance into the little garden, and into the open stall. His brother Jonas was not there. He left a troubled thought to his lost brother, who had, as he still thought, sacrificed himself voluntarily. 'He's rough, but he's noble and brave,' he thought. Then he walked steadily on, at the side of the stranger.

Just behind the market-place they found the horses, as the man had said. They needed no less than three days to reach the border, for they must avoid the railway. Under way it became clear that Shemariah's guide was thoroughly familiar with the country. He made it evident without Shemariah's asking him. He pointed to distant church steeples, and named the villages they belonged to. He named the farms and the estates, and he knew the names of the owners. He often departed from the highroad, and found his way quickly along narrow paths. It was as though he wanted to make Shemariah acquainted with his own country, before the young man departed to visit another.

An hour before midnight they came to the border tavern. It was a quiet night. The tavern stood alone, the only house in the night's stillness, silent, dark, with muffled windows behind which there was no sign of life. About it a thousand crickets chirped unintermittently, the whispering chorus of the night. Otherwise no voice disturbed it. The land was flat; the starry horizon drew a complete circle about it, dark-blue, broken only in the north-east by a light streak, like a blue ring with a setting of silver. One smelled the distant dampness of the swamp, which spread out in the west, and the slow wind which carried the smell over.

'A fine, real summer night,' said Kapturak's courier. And for the first time since they came together he spoke of his business. 'On quiet summer nights like this you can't always pass the border without trouble. For business like ours, rain is better.'

He awakened a little anxiety in Shemariah. Since the tavern before which they stood was closed and silent, he had not thought of its significance until the words of his companion reminded him of their project.

'Let's go in,' he said, speaking as one who will not postpone danger any longer.

'Don't be in a hurry; we will have to wait long enough.'

Nevertheless, he went to the window and knocked lightly on the wooden shutters. The door opened and let a broad stream of yellow light fall over the darkened earth. They entered. Behind the bar, in the midst of the circle of light cast by a hanging lamp, stood the inn-keeper, and nodded at them. On the floor squatted a few men, playing dice. Kapturak sat at a table, with a man in the uniform of a sergeant-major. No one looked up. One heard the rattle of the dice and the tick of the clock on the wall. Shemariah sat down. His companion ordered drinks. Shemariah drank some spirits, he became warm, but quieted. He felt more secure than usual; he knew that he was living through one of those rare moments when a man has as much power over his own destiny as has the great power which conferred it upon him.

Shortly after the clock had struck midnight, a shot resounded, sharp and hard, with a slowly expiring echo. This was the sign which they had decided upon, with which the outpost let it be known that the nightly visit of the border officials was over. The watchman disappeared. Kapturak made a sign to the people to disperse. All rose wearily and shouldered their bundles and luggage. The door opened; one by one they dropped out into the night, and trod their way towards the border. They tried to sing, someone hushed them – it was Kapturak's voice. One did not know from whence it came, from the first rows, from the middle, or from the rear. Thus they walked silently, through the thick chirping of the crickets and the deep blueness of the night. After half an hour, Kapturak's voice commanded them: Lie down!

They fell upon the dew-dampened earth, lay motionless, pressed their pounding hearts against the wet soil, their hearts bidding their homeland farewell. Then someone commanded them to rise. They came to a wide shallow trench; to their left a light was blinking, the light of the sentry hut. Dutifully, but without aiming, the sentry fired a shot after them.

'We are over!' cried a voice.

In this moment, the heavens towards the east lighted up. The men looked backward, towards their homes, over which night seemed to lie, then turned again towards the day, and towards the unknown.

One began to sing; all the others fell in with him. Singing they continued the march. Only Shemariah did not sing with them. He thought about the immediate future (he possessed but two roubles). He thought what the morning at home would be like. In an hour his father would rise, murmur a prayer, clear his throat, gargle, go to the washbowl, and scatter water about. Mother would blow in the samovar. Menuchim would babble something or other into the morning; Miriam would comb the white feathers out of her black hair. Shemariah saw all this more clearly than he had ever seen it when he was still at home and himself a participant in the morning rites. He hardly heard the singing of the others, only his feet took up the rhythm and marched with it.

An hour later he glimpsed the first foreign town, the blue smoke from the first busy smokestacks, a man with a yellow arm-band who received the arrivals. A tower clock struck six.

The wall clock of the Singers also struck six. Mendel arose, gargled, cleared his throat, murmured a morning prayer. Deborah already stood at the stove and blew into the samovar. Menuchim babbled something incoherent in his corner. Miriam combed her hair before the blinded mirror. Then Deborah, still standing at the stove, swallowed her hot tea.

'Where is Shemariah?' she said suddenly. They had all been thinking of him.

'God will help him!' said Mendel Singer. And thus the day began.

And thus began the days which followed, empty days, wretched days. 'A house without children—' thought Deborah. 'I bore them all, I suckled them all, a wind has blown them away.' She looked about for Miriam; she seldom found her daughter at home. Menuchim alone remained for his mother. Whenever she passed his corner he stretched out his arms. And when she kissed him, he sought for her breast, like an infant. She thought reproachfully of the blessing whose fulfilment was so long postponed, and she doubted whether she would live to see the healing of Menuchim.

The house was silent when the sing-song of the studying children ceased. It was silent and gloomy. Winter returned. One had to save oil. One went to bed early.

57

One sank thankfully into the kindly night. From time to time Jonas sent a greeting. He served in Pskov, enjoyed his usual excellent health, and had no trouble with his superiors. Thus the years passed.

VI

ON A LATE summer afternoon a stranger entered the house of Mendel Singer. The door and windows stood open. Black and satiated, the flies stuck motionless to the hot sunny walls, and the sing-song of the scholars streamed out of the open house into the white street. Suddenly they observed the strange man framed in the doorway and became dumb. Deborah got up from her stool. Miriam hurried across from the other side of the street holding the wobbling Menuchim firmly by the hand. Mendel Singer stood before the stranger and measured him with his glance.

He was an extraordinary man. He wore a wide black hat, light-coloured flapping trousers, good yellow boots, and over his bright green shirt a shrill red cravat floated like a flag. Without moving he said something, obviously a greeting, in an unintelligible language. It sounded as though he spoke with a cherry in his mouth. And furthermore green stems were sticking out of his coat pocket. His smooth long upper lip raised itself slowly like a curtain and revealed strong yellow teeth reminiscent of a horse. The children laughed, and even Mendel Singer grinned. The stranger pulled out a letter folded lengthwise and read the address and the names of the Singers in his peculiar fashion, so that everybody laughed again.

'America!' cried the man finally and handed Mendel Singer a letter. Happy anticipation awoke in Mendel and shone in his face.

'Shemariah,' he said. With a gesture of his hand he dismissed the scholars, as one shoos away flies. They ran out. The stranger seated himself. Deborah set tea, preserves, lemonade upon the table. Mendel opened the letter. Deborah and Miriam also sat down. And Singer began to read the following:

'Dear Father, beloved Mother, dear Miriam, and my good Menuchim! I don't address Jonas because he is with the soldiers. Also I beg you not to send this letter to him directly, because he might have unpleasant difficulties if he is found corresponding with a brother who is a deserter. That's why I've waited so long and have not written you through the post, until I finally had an opportunity to send you this letter with my good friend Mac. He knows all about you through the tales I have told him, but he won't be able to speak a word with you, because he's not only an American but his parents were born in America, and also he's not a Jew. But he's better than ten Jews.

'Well, I must begin to tell you all about everything from the beginning until now: First, when I got over the border, I had nothing to eat, only two roubles in my pocket, but I thought to myself, God will provide. A man came along from a Trieste shipping company, he had on an official cap and he had to bring us from the border. There were twelve men of us, the other eleven all had some money; they bought themselves forged papers and steamship tickets, and the agent of the shipping company took them to the train. I went along. I thought to myself, it can't do any harm. I'll go along and in any case I'll see how one gets to go to America. So when I stayed back with the agent, he was surprised that I didn't travel with the others. "I haven't got a kopek," I said to the agent. He asked whether I could read or write. "A little," I said, "but perhaps not enough." Well, to make a long story short, the man had a job for me. Every day when the deserters arrived, I had to go to the border, fetch them, buy everything for them, and talk them into believing that America was a land flowing with milk and honey. Well, I began to work, and fifty per cent of everything I earned I had to give to the agent because I was only a sub-agent. He wore a cap with the firm's name on it in gold

61

embroidery, but I just had an arm-band. After two months I told him I had to get sixty per cent or I'd throw up the job. He gave sixty. To make a long story short, I got acquainted with a pretty girl where I lived; Vega was her name, and now she's your daughter-in-law. Her father gave us some money so that I could go into business, but I never could forget how the other eleven went to America and how I alone remained behind. So I said good-bye to Vega. I knew all about ships – after all it was my trade – and so I went to America. And here I am. Vega came two months ago; we've gotten married and we're very happy. Mac has the pictures in his pocket. First I sewed buttons on pants, then I ironed pants, then I sewed the lining in the sleeves, and pretty soon I was almost a tailor, like all Jews in America. But then I met Mac on a ferry boat to Staten Island, going to Fort Lafayette. When you get here I'll show you the place. From then on I began to work with him at all sorts of businesses. Finally we took up insurance. I insure the Jews and he the Irish. I've even insured a few Christians. Mac will give you ten dollars from me. You buy something with it for the journey. Because soon, with God's help, I'll send you steamship tickets.

    'I embrace and kiss you all.
      Your son,
        Shemariah
        (here I'm called Sam).'

When Mendel Singer had finished the letter there was a vibrant silence in the room that seemed to melt into the stillness of the late summer afternoon, and out of which all the members of the family seemed to hear the voice of the emigrant son. Yes, Shemariah himself spoke over there in faraway America, where in this hour it was perhaps night or morning. For a moment they all forgot Mac's presence. It was as though he had become invisible behind the distant Shemariah. He was like a messenger who delivers a letter, goes on, and disappears. He himself had to remind them of his presence.

He got up and reached into his trousers pockets like a magician who begins to conjure something. He brought out a pocketbook, and took out of it ten dollars and two photographs. One depicted Shemariah with his wife Vega on a bench in a park, and in the other he was alone in a bathing suit on a beach, one body and one face among a dozen bodies and faces, no longer Shemariah but a Sam.

The stranger handed the money and the pictures to Deborah, after he had looked them all over as if to assure himself that each one of them believed in his trustworthiness. She held the note folded in one hand; with the other she put the pictures on the table beside the letter. All this lasted a few moments, in which everybody remained silent.

Finally, Mendel Singer laid his index finger upon the photographs and said: 'That is Shemariah!'

'Shemariah!' repeated the others. And even Menuchim who now reached above the table gave a clear whinny, and cast one of his shy glances upon the pictures, with cross-eyed cautiousness.

Suddenly it seemed to Mendel Singer as though the stranger was no longer a stranger and as though he understood the same speech.

'Tell me something!' he said to Mac.

And the American as though he had understood Mendel's words, began to move his great mouth and to recount something unintelligible with gay energy, and spoke the words as though he were chewing something good with relish. He told the Singers that he had come to Russia to do some business with hops because he was thinking of starting a brewery in Chicago, but the Singers did not understand. Now that he was here he certainly didn't want to miss visiting the Caucasus and he especially wanted to climb Mount Ararat because he had read about it in the Bible. The audience strained themselves to listen to Mac's account, hoping that they would catch a single tiny intelligible syllable out of the storm of words, and their hearts leaped at the word Ararat which sounded strangely familiar to them although he had changed it dismayingly and rolled it out with a dangerous and terrible rumble.

Mendel Singer alone could not stop smiling. He liked to hear the language which had now become that of his son Shemariah, and while Mac talked Mendel tried to imagine how the son looked when he also spoke such words. Presently it seemed to him as though the voice of his own son spoke out of the gaily grinding mill of the stranger's mouth.

The American ended his talk, went around the table, and pressed everybody heartily by the hand. He lifted Menuchim swiftly in the air; observed the distorted head, the thin neck, the blue, lifeless hands, and the crooked legs; and set him upon the ground with a tender and considerate contempt, as though he wished to express the idea that strange creatures like this should cower on the earth and not stand at tables. Then he went out through the open door, tall, broad, swaying a little as he walked, his hands in his trousers pockets, with the whole family crowding after him. They all shaded their eyes with their hands, looking into the sunny street through the midst of which strode Mac, and at the end of which he stopped again for a moment to wave back.

For a long time they stayed outside, even after Mac had disappeared. They held their hands above their eyes and gazed into the dust-laden rays of the sun on the empty street.

Finally Deborah said, 'Well, he's gone!' And as though the stranger had just then disappeared, they all turned and stood each with his arm about another's shoulder before the photographs on the table.

'How much are ten dollars?' asked Miriam and began to count up.

'It doesn't matter,' said Deborah, 'how much ten dollars are. We certainly won't buy ourselves anything with it.'

'Why not?' asked Miriam. 'Shall we travel in these rags?'

'Who's travelling and where?' cried the mother.

'To America,' said Miriam and smiled. 'Sam wrote it himself.'

For the first time a member of the family had called Shemariah Sam, and it was as though Miriam had intentionally used the American name of her brother in order to lend emphasis to his demand that the family should come to America.

'Sam!' cried Mendel Singer. 'Who is Sam?'

'Yes,' echoed Deborah. 'Who is Sam?'

'Sam,' said Miriam, still smiling, 'is my brother in America and your son!'

The parents were silent. Suddenly Menuchim's voice sounded clearly out of the corner into which he had crept.

'Menuchim can't go!' said Deborah gently, as though she feared that the sick child might understand.

'Menuchim can't go!' repeated Mendel Singer just as softly.

The sun seemed to sink rapidly. They all stared through the open window at the wall of the house across the way, upon which the black shadows rose visibly as a lake rises over its boundaries with the beginning of a flood. A faint wind stirred and the shutters rattled in their hinges.

'Close the door, there's a draught!' said Deborah.

Miriam went to the door. Before she touched the latch she stood still a second and looked through the door in the direction in which Mac had disappeared. Then Miriam banged the door to and said, 'That's the wind.'

Mendel stood at the window. He saw how the evening shadows crept up the wall. He lifted his head and observed how the sun gilded the ridge-pole of the house across the street. He stood for a long time thus, the room, his wife, his daughter Miriam, and the sick Menuchim at his back. He felt all of them and was conscious of every move. He knew that Deborah laid her head on the table in order to weep, that Miriam turned her face towards the stove, and that her shoulders shook now and then, although she did not weep at all. He knew that his wife was only waiting for the moment when he would seize his prayer book, in order to go into the house of prayer for the evening service, and Miriam would take up her shawl to hurry across to the neighbours. Then Deborah would bury the ten-dollar note under the floor-board.

When he stepped upon it, it creakingly betrayed the secret which it covered, and reminded him of the growling of the dogs which Sameshkin kept chained before his door. He knew that floor-board, did Mendel Singer. And in order not to think of Sameshkin's black dogs, which were terrifying to him, living symbols of sin, he always avoided stepping on the board, unless he happened to forget it as he walked up and down through the room, zealous in giving instruction. Now, as he watched the gold strips of sunshine become smaller and smaller and slip from the ridge-pole of the house to the roof and from there to the white chimney, he believed, for the first time in his life, that he clearly felt the crafty, soundless skulking of the day, the treacherous deception

67

of the eternal change, of day and night, summer and winter, and life, that ran along in the same groove, monotonous despite all its terrors, anticipated or unexpected. These terrors grew only upon the changeful banks of life's stream; Mendel Singer tramped past them.

A man came out of America, laughed, brought a letter, dollars, and pictures of Shemariah, and vanished again into the veiled distance. The sons disappeared. Jonas served the Tsar in Pskov, and was no longer Jonas. Shemariah bathed on an ocean strand and no longer was called Shemariah. Miriam gazed after the American, and wanted to go to America, too. Only Menuchim remained what he had always been since the day of his birth – a cripple. And Mendel Singer remained what he had always been – a teacher.

The narrow street darkened completely, and came to life at the same time. The fat wife of Chaim, the glazier, and the ninety-year-old grandmother of the long dead locksmith, Yossel Kopp, fetched chairs out of their houses, in order to sit before their doorsteps and enjoy the fresh evening air. Black and hurrying, the Jews hastened to the synagogue, with curt murmured greetings. Then Mendel Singer turned around; it was also time for him to go. He passed Deborah, whose head still rested on the hard table. Her face, that Mendel Singer had been unable, for years, to stand the sight of, was buried now, as though planted in the hard wood, and the darkness which began to fill the room also covered the hardness and the shyness of Mendel Singer. His hand caressed the broad back of his wife. Once this flesh had been familiar to him; it was strange to him now.

She raised herself and said, 'You are going to your prayers!' And because she was thinking of something else, she turned the phrase around, and said in an absent-minded voice, 'To your prayers, you are going!'

Miriam in her yellow shawl left the house at the same time as her father, and went to the neighbours.

It was the first week in the month of Ab. The Jews assembled after evening prayers to greet the new moon, and, because the night was pleasant and refreshing after the hot day, they followed more willingly and believingly than usual the commandment of God to welcome the rebirth of the moon in an open place, over which the heavens could arch more widely than over the narrow streets of the little town. They hurried on, silent and black, in irregular groups, behind the houses; saw in the distance the forest, dark and silent as themselves but eternal in its deep-rootedness; saw the veils of night above the broad fields. Finally they stopped. They gazed at the heavens and sought for the silver curve of the new satellite that today should be born again as on the day of its creation. They closed their ranks, opened their prayer books – the pages shimmered white, the angular letters stood out black in the blue night light – and began to murmur the greeting to the moon, rocking their bodies to and fro, so that they looked as though shaken by an invisible wind. They swayed ever more rapidly; their prayers came louder and louder; they flung the native, primeval words aggressively at the distant skies. The earth on which they stood was alien to them; the forest stared back at them with enmity; the barking of the dogs, whose suspicious ears they had awakened, was full of malice. Only in the moon did they feel confidence, the moon, born today in this world as it had been in the land of their fathers, and in the Lord, who watched over all, at home and in exile.

With a loud 'Amen' they closed the blessing, extended their hands to each other, and wished each other a happy month, prosperity in business, and health for the sickly. They parted; one by one they walked home, disappearing behind the little doors of their crooked houses. Only one Jew remained behind, Mendel Singer.

His companions had taken leave of him only a few minutes before, but it seemed to him that he had stood there for an hour. He breathed in the undisturbed peace of the open, took a few steps forward, felt tired, had the desire to lay himself upon the ground, but felt nervous about the unknown earth and the dangerous snakes which probably were hidden about. He thought of his lost son Jonas. Jonas slept in a barracks now, on the hay, in a stall, probably next to horses. His son Shemariah lived on the other side of the water. Who was farther away, Jonas or Shemariah? There at home Deborah had the dollars hidden, and Miriam was telling the neighbours, now, about the visit of the American.

The young sickle moon was already spreading a strong silver light. Faithfully accompanied by the brightest star of the heavens she sailed through the night.

Sometimes the dogs howled and frightened Mendel. They tore at the peace of the earth and increased Mendel Singer's unrest. Although he was only five minutes away from the houses of the town, he seemed to himself infinitely distant from the inhabited world of the Jews, indescribably alone, threatened by dangers, and yet incapable of going back.

He turned northward. There breathed the dark forest. To the right the swamp, with a few isolated, silvery willows, stretched away for many versts. To the left lay fields, under opal veils.

Sometimes Mendel thought he heard human sounds coming from an uncertain direction. He heard familiar voices, and it almost seemed to him as though he understood what they said. Then he remembered that he had heard them long ago, that he was listening to an echo which had long been waiting in his memory.

Suddenly there was a rustling to the left, in the wheat, although no wind stirred. The rustling seemed closer. Now Mendel could also see how the man-high ears of wheat moved. Something must be slinking amongst them, a human being, a huge animal, perhaps a monster. It would have been well to run away, but Mendel waited and prepared for death. A peasant or a soldier would now emerge from the grain, accuse Mendel of theft, and beat him then and there – stone him, perhaps. Or it might be a tramp, a murderer, a criminal, who would not wish to be seen or heard. 'Almighty God!' whispered Mendel.

Then he heard voices. There were two of them, who

passed through the grain, and that it was not one quieted the Jew, although he said to himself that there might well be two murderers. No, they were not murderers, but lovers. A girl's voice spoke. A man laughed. Even lovers could be dangerous. There were many cases where a man had become furious when he caught a witness of his love affair. Soon they must emerge from the field. Mendel Singer overcame his terrified disgust of snakes, and softly lay down, his eyes turned towards the wheat. Then the ears parted; the man emerged first, a man in uniform, a soldier in a dark-blue cap, booted and spurred, the metal shining and clinking softly. Behind him a yellow shawl gleamed, a yellow shawl, a yellow shawl. A voice arose, the voice of the girl. The soldier turned, laid his arm about her shoulders; now the shawl parted, the soldier went behind the girl, his hands held her breasts, she sank back against him.

Mendel Singer closed his eyes, and let the catastrophe pass by him in darkness. If he had not feared to reveal himself, he would have stopped his ears also, in order not to hear. But as it was he had to hear: dreadful words, the silver clink of spurs, suppressed, senseless giggles, and a deep laugh from the man. Now, with longing, he awaited the yapping of the dogs. If only they would howl loudly, very loudly. If only murderers would come out of the wheat, to attack him! The voices became more distant. Everything was gone. Nothing had been.

Mendel Singer stood up hurriedly, looked round about him, lifted with both hands the skirts of his long coat, and fled in the direction of the town. The shutters were closed, but many women sat before the doors and gossiped or called to each other stridently. He slowed his walk, in order not to attract attention; but he took long strides, his coat skirts still in his hands. He stopped before his own house. He knocked on the window. Deborah opened it.

'Where is Miriam?' asked Mendel.

'She has gone for a walk,' said Deborah. 'You can't hold her any longer. Day and night she goes walking. She is hardly in the house for half an hour. God has punished me with these children. Did anyone ever in this world—'

'Be quiet,' Mendel Singer interrupted her. 'When Miriam comes home, say that I was asking for her. I shall not come home tonight, only tomorrow morning. Today is the anniversary of the death of my grandfather Zallel. I go to pray.'

And he departed without waiting for an answer from his wife.

It could hardly have been three hours since he had left the synagogue. Now that he entered it again, it seemed to him as though he had returned there after many weeks, and he stroked with a tender hand the lid of his old prayer desk and celebrated a homecoming with it. He lifted the lid and reached for his old, black, heavy book, which felt so at home in his hands that he would have recognized it instantly, without hesitation, among a thousand similar books. So familiar to him was the leathern smoothness of the binding, with the round, raised little islands of tallow, the encrusted remains of

73

innumerable candles burned long ago; so familiar the under corners of the pages, yellowish, porous, greasy, thrice curled by a decade of turning them with moistened fingers. Any prayer that he needed at the moment he could turn to immediately. It was buried in his memory with the smallest feature of that physiognomy which it carried in this book, the number of the line, the character and size of the print, and the exact colour tone of the page.

It was twilight in the synagogue. The yellow light of the candles on the eastern wall, next to the cabinet with the Torah rolls, did not dismiss the darkness, but seemed rather to bury itself in it. Through the window one saw the heavens, and a few stars. One could recognize all the objects in the room, the desks, pews, the table, the benches, the paper shavings on the floor, the candelabra on the walls, a few covers with golden fringes. Mendel Singer lighted two candles, stuck them fast to the naked wood of his desk, shut his eyes, and began to pray. With closed eyes he knew where a page came to an end, and mechanically turned to the next. Gradually his torso slipped into the old, customary swaying, his whole body prayed with him, the feet scraped the floor, the hands closed to fists and pounded like hammers on the desk, on his breast, on the book, and in the air. On the stove bench slept a homeless Jew. His breathing accompanied and supported Mendel Singer's monotonous song, which was like a hot chant in the yellow desert, lost, and familiar with death.

His own voice and the breathing of the sleeper

numbed Mendel, drove every thought out of his heart; he was nothing more than a man praying; the words passed through him to Heaven; he was a hollow vessel, a funnel for prayer. So his prayers went out to meet the morning.

Day breathed on the windows. The lights faltered and dimmed. Behind the low huts one saw the sun rise, filling with red flames the two eastern windows of the room. Mendel extinguished the candles, put away the book, opened his eyes, and turned to go. He walked into the open air. It smelled of summer, dry swamps, and awakened green. The shutters were still closed. People slept.

Mendel knocked three times with his hand upon his door. He was strong and fresh, as though he had slept dreamlessly and long. He knew exactly what he must do. Deborah opened the door.

'Make me some tea,' said Mendel. 'Then I have something to say to you. Is Miriam at home?'

'Of course,' said Deborah, 'where else should she be? Do you think she is already in America?'

The samovar hummed; Deborah breathed into a drinking glass and polished it brightly. Then Mendel and Deborah drank together, with pursed, sipping lips. Suddenly Mendel set down his glass and said:

'We will go to America. Menuchim must remain behind. We must take Miriam with us. Misfortune hangs over us if we stay.'

He was quiet for a moment and then said softly:

'She is going with a Cossack.'

The glass fell ringing from Deborah's hand.

Miriam awoke in the corner, and Menuchim moved in his heavy sleep. Then all was still. Above the house, under the skies, a million larks were trilling.

With a bright flash the rising sun struck the window, lit the polished tin of the samovar, and transformed it into a curved mirror.

Thus the day began.

VII

ONE TRAVELLED TO Dubno with Sameshkin's wagon; one travelled to Moscow by railway; but in order to get to America one travelled not only with a ship, but with documents. And in order to get these one had to go to Dubno.

And so Deborah betook herself to Sameshkin. Sameshkin no longer sat upon the stove bench; he was never at home at all. Moreover it was Thursday, the day of the pig market, and Sameshkin would not be home for an hour.

Deborah walked up and down, up and down, before Sameshkin's hut and thought only about America.

A dollar is more than two roubles, a rouble is a hundred kopeks, two roubles are two hundred kopeks, how many kopeks in heaven's name are there in a dollar?

77

Furthermore how many dollars will Shemariah send? America, how blessed is that country!

Miriam was going with a Cossack. In Russia she could do that, but in America there were no Cossacks.

Russia is a sad country, America is a free country, a happy country, a gay country. Mendel would no longer be a teacher; the father of a rich son, that's what he'd be.

It was not one hour, it was not two hours, it was fully three hours before Deborah heard Sameshkin's nailed boots.

It was evening, but still hot. The declining sun was already golden, but he would not yet yield, he sank very slowly. Deborah sweated from heat, from excitement, and from a hundred unusual thoughts.

Now, as Sameshkin approached, she became even warmer. He wore a heavy cap of bearskin, rough, and mangy in places, and a short fur jacket over dirty linen trousers which were stuck into heavy boots, but he did not sweat at all.

The moment Deborah saw him she also smelled him, because he stank of brandy. A nice time she would have with him. It was no picnic handling even a sober Sameshkin.

On Monday the pig market would be in Dubno. It was too bad that Sameshkin had already attended the pig market at home. He would have no reason for going to Dubno, and the journey would cost money.

Deborah met Sameshkin in the middle of the street. He reeled; only his heavy boots kept him upright. Lucky that he's not bare-footed! thought Deborah, not without malice.

Sameshkin did not recognize the woman who blocked his way. 'Out of the way with females!' he cried, and made a gesture with his hand, half grabbing, half striking at her.

'It's me!' said Deborah bravely. 'Monday we're going to Dubno!'

'God bless you!' cried Sameshkin in a friendly tone. He stopped, and braced himself with his elbow on Deborah's shoulder. She was afraid to move lest Sameshkin should fall.

Sameshkin weighed a good hundred and sixty pounds; his whole weight rested upon his elbow, and this elbow rested upon Deborah's shoulder.

This was the first time a strange man had ever been so close to her. She was frightened, but at the same time she thought of how old she was. She also thought of Miriam's Cossack and how long it had been since Mendel last touched her.

'Yes, sweetheart,' said Sameshkin. 'Monday we will go to Dubno, and on the way we'll sleep together.'

'Shame on you, old man,' said Deborah. 'I'll tell your wife. I suppose you're drunk.'

'Drunk he is not,' replied Sameshkin, 'but drunk he has. What in the world do you want to do in Dubno if you don't sleep with Sameshkin?'

'Get documents,' said Deborah. 'We are going to America.'

'The trip will cost fifty kopeks if you don't sleep with

him and thirty if you do. He will make you a little baby and you'll get it in America to remember Sameshkin by.'

Deborah shuddered in the midst of the heat.

Nevertheless, after a moment's pause, she said, 'I won't sleep with you and I'll pay thirty-five kopeks.'

Sameshkin freed himself suddenly. He took his elbow off Deborah's shoulders. It seemed that he had become sober.

'Thirty-five kopeks!' he said in a firm voice.

'Monday morning at five.'

'Monday morning at five.'

Sameshkin turned in at his house and Deborah went slowly homeward.

The sun had gone down. The wind was from the west, violet clouds were piling up on the horizon, tomorrow it would rain. Deborah thought: Tomorrow it will rain, and felt a rheumatic twinge in her knee. She greeted it, her loyal old enemy. One gets old, she thought. Women get old faster than men. Sameshkin is as old as I, even older. Miriam is young, she goes with a Cossack.

At the word Cossack, which she uttered aloud, Deborah started. It was as though the sound made her for the first time aware of the dreadfulness of the state of affairs.

At home she saw her daughter Miriam and her husband Mendel. They sat at the table, the father and the daughter, and they were so stubbornly silent that Deborah knew as she entered that it was already an old silence, a settled, domestic silence.

'I have talked with Sameshkin,' began Deborah. 'I

start for Dubno Monday at five in the morning to get the documents. He wants thirty-five kopeks.' And because she was ridden by the devil of vanity she added: 'He takes only me so cheaply!'

'You can't go alone, anyway,' said Mendel Singer with weariness in his voice and dread in his heart. 'I have talked with many Jews who know all about it. They say that I must appear in person before the *uriadnik.*'

'You before the *uriadnik?*'

It was really not simple to imagine Mendel Singer in an office. Never in his life had he spoken with a *uriadnik.* He had never met a policeman without trembling. He carefully avoided uniformed men, horses, and dogs. Mendel should speak with the *uriadnik?*

'Don't mix in with things that you can only mess up, Mendel,' said Deborah. 'I'll fix everything myself.'

'All Jews,' insisted Mendel, 'have told me that I must appear personally.'

'Then we will go together on Monday!'

'And where will Menuchim be?'

'Miriam will stay with him!'

Mendel looked at his wife. He sought, with his glance, to catch her eyes, which hid themselves fearfully under her lids. Miriam, who watched the table from her corner, caught her father's glance, and her heart beat faster. Monday she had a rendezvous. She had a rendezvous on Monday. She had a rendezvous for the whole hot midsummer. Her love blossomed late, among the high ears of the wheat. Miriam feared the harvest. Already she sometimes heard the peasants preparing for it, whetting their scythes on the blue grindstones. Where could they go when the fields were bare? She must go to America. She had a vague picture of freer love in America, among the tall houses that hid one better than the ears of corn in the field, and this comforted her about the approach of the harvest. It would be here soon. Miriam had no time to lose. She loved Stepan. He would stay behind. She loved all men; storms broke from them, their violent hands kindled flames in the heart which only they could quiet. The men were called Stepan – Ivan – Vsevolod. But in America there were many more men.

'I don't want to stay alone in the house,' said Miriam. 'I'm afraid.'

'We ought to put a Cossack in the house for her, to guard her,' Mendel could not keep from saying.

Miriam reddened. She thought that her father saw her blushes, although she stood in the corner, in the shadow. Her blushes must shine through the darkness; Miriam's face glowed like a red lamp. She covered it with her hands, and broke into tears.

'Go on out,' said Deborah. 'Close the shutters. It is late.'

She felt her way out, cautiously, her hands still before her eyes. Outside she stopped a moment. All the stars of heaven stood there, near, and alive, as though they had awaited Miriam before the house. Their clear golden splendour contained all the glory of the great free world; they were tiny mirrors, in which the wonder of America was reflected.

She went to the window, looked in, trying to discover from the mien of her parents what they spoke about. She released the shutters from the iron hooks that held them back, and closed both wings, as one closes a cupboard. She thought of a coffin. She buried her parents in the little house. She felt no sorrow. Mendel and Deborah Singer were buried. The world was wide and full of life. Stepan, Ivan, and Vsevolod were alive. America was alive, on the other side of the great water, with all its tall houses and its millions of men.

As she re-entered the room, her father Mendel Singer said, 'She can't even close the blinds! She needs half an hour to do it!'

He groaned, rose, and walked to the wall on which a small oil lamp was hanging, with a dark-blue base and a sooty chimney, bound by a rusty wire to a round cracked mirror whose function it was to strengthen, without extra cost, the meagre light. The upper opening of the chimney was higher than Mendel Singer's head. In vain he tried to blow out the light. He stood on his toes, he blew, but the wick only flared up the more strongly.

Meanwhile Deborah lighted a small, yellowish taper and stood it on the tiles of the stove. Mendel, groaning, climbed upon a stool, and finally blew the lamp out. Miriam lay down in a corner, next to Menuchim. She would wait until it was dark to undress. She waited breathless, with closed eyelids, until her father had murmured his night prayers. Through a round knothole in the shutters she saw the blue and gold shimmer of the night. She undressed and felt her breasts. They hurt her.

Her skin had its own memory, and remembered in many places the great, hard, hot hands of the men. Her sense of smell had its own memory and retained with torturing fidelity the odour of men's sweat, of brandy and of leather.

She heard the snoring of her parents, and Menuchim's rattling breath. Then Miriam arose, barefoot, in her chemise, with her heavy braids hanging forward over her shoulders and reaching to her thighs. She pushed back the bolt and stepped out, into the strange night. She breathed deeply. It seemed to her that she breathed in the entire night; all the golden stars she swallowed with her breath, and always more and more stars burned in the heavens.

Frogs croaked and crickets chirped; the north-east sky was rimmed with a silver stripe, in which the morning already seemed to be contained. Miriam thought of the cornfield, her marriage bed. She went around the house. There, shimmering in the distance, she saw the great white wall of the barracks. They sent a few meagre lights towards Miriam. In a great room slept Stepan, Ivan, and Vsevolod, and many other men.

Tomorrow was Friday. Everything must be prepared for Saturday: the meat balls, the pike, the chicken soup. Baking began at six in the morning. As the wide silver stripe reddened, Miriam slunk back into the room. She did not sleep again. Through the knothole in the shutters she saw the first flames of the sun. Already her father and mother moved in their sleep. Morning had come.

The Sabbath passed. Miriam spent Sunday in the cornfield, with Stepan. In the end they went a long way off, to the next village. Miriam drank spirits. At home, they looked for her the whole day long. Let them look! Her life was precious, the summer was short, soon the harvest would begin.

In the forest she lay once again with Stepan. Tomorrow, Monday, her father would go to Dubno, to get his papers.

At five o'clock on Monday morning, Mendel Singer arose. He drank tea, prayed, then laid the phylacteries away quickly and went to Sameshkin.

'Good morning,' he called, while he was still a long way off. It was as though Mendel Singer already began to negotiate with the authorities, before he even entered Sameshkin's wagon, and as though he must treat Sameshkin like an *uriadnik*.

'I'd rather go with your wife!' said Sameshkin. 'She's still good-looking for her years, and has a decent bosom.'

'Let us start,' said Mendel.

The horses whinnied, and switched their hind parts with their tails. 'Hai! Vyo!' cried Sameshkin, and cracked his whip.

At eleven o'clock in the morning they came to Dubno.

Mendel had to wait. He stepped, his cap in his hand, through the great door. The porter carried a sabre.

'Where do you want to go?' he asked.

'I want to go to America. What must I do?'

'What is your name?'

'Mendel Mechelovich Singer.'

'Why do you want to go to America?'

'To earn money; I am badly off.'

'You go to number eighty-four,' said the porter. 'There are many waiting there already.'

They sat in a great, vaulted corridor, tinted a mustard colour. Men in blue uniforms were on guard before the door. All along the walls stood brown benches – all the benches were occupied. But as soon as a newcomer arrived, the men in blue uniforms made a motion of the hand, and the occupants crowded together, and each time made a new place. They smoked, spat, cracked squash seeds, and snored. The day here was no day. Through the opaque glass of a high, very distant skylight, one got a pale apprehension of day. Clocks ticked somewhere but they seemed to go along independently of time, which in these high corridors stood still.

Sometimes a man in a blue uniform called out a name. All the sleepers awakened. The one called rose, scrambled towards the door, pulled his clothes into order, and walked through one of the high double doors which had a round white button in the place of a latch.

Mendel considered how he would handle this button in order to open the door. He stood up. His limbs ached from long sitting crowded in amongst the others. Hardly had he risen, when one of the blue uniforms approached him.

'*Sidai!*' called the blue man. 'Sit down, you!'

Mendel Singer no longer found a place on the bench. He stood beside it, pressed himself against the wall, and wished he could become as flat as the wall.

'Are you waiting for number eighty-four?' asked the blue man.

'Yes,' said Mendel. He was convinced now that they intended to throw him out. Deborah would have to come. Fifty kopeks plus fifty make a rouble.

But the blue man had no intention of throwing Mendel out. The blue man set great store by having all the waiting crowd in their places where he could observe them. If one stood up, he might be preparing to throw a bomb. Anarchists sometimes disguised themselves, thought the man at the door. And he beckoned Mendel to come to him, felt him over, asked for his papers. When he found everything in order and saw that Mendel had no place to sit, the blue man said: 'Listen. You see that glass door? Open that. There is number eighty-four.'

'What are you after here?' yelled a broad-shouldered man who was sitting behind a desk. The official sat directly under the picture of the Tsar. He consisted of a moustache, a bald head, epaulets, and buttons. He was like a fine bust, behind his marble ink-stand.

'Who let you come in here like that? Why didn't you have yourself announced?' rumbled a voice out of the bust.

Mendel Singer bowed himself to the ground. He was not prepared for such a reception. He bowed and let the thunder roll over his back; he wished he could become infinitesimal, one with the earth. It was as though a storm had overtaken him in an open field. The folds of his long coat parted, and the official saw a bit of Mendel Singer's threadbare trousers, and the scuffed leather of his boot shafts. The sight made the official milder.

'Come here,' he commanded, and Mendel drew nearer, his head pushed forward, as though he would beat it against the writing-desk. Only when he saw that he was reaching the hem of the carpet, did Mendel lift his head a little. The official smiled.

'Let me see your papers,' he said.

Then it was quiet. One heard the ticking of the clock. Through Venetian blinds the golden light of late afternoon shone. The papers rustled. Once the official meditated, gazed into the air, and suddenly swatted a fly with his hand. He held the tiny animal in his huge fist, opened his hand cautiously, pulled off a wing, then another, and watched for a second how the crippled insect crept about the desk.

'The petition?' he asked suddenly. 'Where is the petition?'

'I cannot write Russian, your Excellency,' Mendel excused himself.

'I know that, you idiot. Sure you can't write! I didn't ask for testimonials of your writing ability, but for the petition. And why do we keep a writer? Eh? On the parterre floor? In number three? Eh? For you, you ass, just because you can't write. So go to number three. Write the petition. Say I sent you, so you won't have to wait, and will be taken care of immediately. Then come back to me. But tomorrow. And tomorrow afternoon, as far as I am concerned, you can leave.'

Once again Mendel bowed low. He walked out backwards, he dared not turn his back on the official, and the way to the door seemed to him infinitely long. He thought he had walked for an hour. At last he felt the door. He turned hastily, grasped the knob, turned it first left, then right. Then he bowed once more. At last he stood again in the corridor.

In number three sat an ordinary official, without epaulets. It was a low, stuffy room. Many people stood about the table. The clerk wrote and wrote, jabbing the pen each time impatiently into the bottom of the ink-well. He wrote briskly, but he was never finished. New people came all the time. And yet he found time to notice Mendel.

'His Excellency, the gentleman in number eighty-four, sent me,' said Mendel.

'Come here,' said the clerk.

They made room for Mendel Singer.

'One rouble for the stamp!' said the clerk. Mendel fished a rouble out of his blue handkerchief. It was a hard, shiny rouble. The clerk did not take the rouble. He expected another fifty kopeks, at least. Mendel did not understand the rather apparent wish of the clerk.

Then the clerk was angry.

'Are those papers!' he cried. 'They're rags! They fall to pieces in one's hands!' And he tore one of the documents, as though by accident. It fell into two parts, and the official reached for the paste-pot to stick it together again. Mendel Singer trembled.

The paste was dry. The official spat into the bottle, then he breathed on it. But it stayed dry. Suddenly he had an idea. One saw in his face that he had an idea. He opened a drawer, shoved Mendel Singer's papers into it, closed it again, tore a little green slip from a pad of paper, stamped it, gave it to Mendel, and said:

'I'll tell you what. You come back tomorrow morning at ten o'clock! Then we will be alone. Then we can talk with each other in peace. Leave your papers with me. You can get them tomorrow morning. Just show the slip.'

Mendel left. Sameshkin was waiting outside. He sat beside his horses, on a stone. The sun was setting. Evening had come.

'We don't go until tomorrow,' said Mendel. 'I've got to come back at ten in the morning.'

He sought for a synagogue, where he might spend the night. He bought some bread and two onions, stuck everything in his pocket, stopped a Jew and asked him where the synagogue was.

'We'll go together,' said the Jew.

On the way Mendel told him his story.

'Among us, in the synagogue,' said the Jew, 'you will find a man who will take care of the whole matter for you. He has already sent lots of Jews to America. Do you know Kapturak?'

'Kapturak? Of course! He got my son over!'

'Old clients!' said Kapturak. In the late summer he

stayed in Dubno; he served in the synagogue. 'That time before, your wife came to see me. I still remember your son. He's had good luck, eh? Kapturak has a lucky hand.'

It came out that Kapturak was prepared to take over the arrangements. For the time being, his price was ten roubles per head. Mendel could not pay an advance of ten roubles. Kapturak knew a way. He got the address of young Singer. In four weeks he would have an answer and money, if the son really intended to bring his parents over.

'Give me your green slip, the letter from America, and depend on me!' said Kapturak. And the bystanders nodded. 'You go on home today. In a few days I'll be coming your way. Depend upon Kapturak!'

A few bystanders repeated, 'Depend upon Kapturak!'

'It's great luck that I met you here,' said Mendel.

All of them shook hands with him and wished him a good journey. He returned to the market-place where Sameshkin was waiting. Sameshkin was just about to go to sleep in his wagon.

'Only the Devil can make sure arrangements with a Jew,' he said. 'Well, let's start.'

They started.

Sameshkin bound the reins around his wrists. He hoped to snooze a little. He actually did nod; the horses shied at the shadow of a scarecrow, which some mischievous youngsters had taken from a field and set at the side of the road. The animals broke into a gallop, the wagon seemed to raise itself into the air. Soon, thought

Mendel, it would begin to flap wings. And his heart galloped, also, as though it would like to leave his breast and leap away.

Suddenly Sameshkin uttered a loud curse. The wagon skidded into a ditch; the horses still scrambled with their front feet on the road. Sameshkin lay on Mendel Singer.

They clambered up again. The axle was splintered, a wheel had become loose, another had lost two spokes. They would have to spend the night here. Tomorrow they would see . . .

'So your journey to America begins!' said Sameshkin. 'Why do you people always go wandering around in the world! The Devil drives you from one place to another. Our sort stay where they are born; only when there's a war, we go to Japan.'

Mendel Singer was silent. He sat by the roadside, next to Sameshkin. For the first time in his life, Mendel Singer sat on the naked earth, in the middle of the wild night, beside a peasant. Above him he saw the heavens and the stars, and he thought: They conceal God. All this the Lord created in six days. And if a Jew wants to go to America, it takes years!

'Do you see how beautiful the country is?' asked Sameshkin. 'Soon the harvest will come. It is a good year. If everything goes as I expect, I'll buy me a new horse in the autumn. Do you hear from your son Jonas? He understands horses. He's entirely different from you. Did your wife ever deceive you?'

'Everything is possible,' Mendel replied. He felt suddenly unburdened; he could comprehend everything;

the night freed him from prejudices. He even drew up close to Sameshkin, as to a brother.

'Everything is possible,' he said. 'Women don't amount to much.'

Suddenly Mendel began to sob. Mendel wept, in the midst of the strange night, next to Sameshkin.

The peasant pressed his fists in his eyes, because he felt that he too would weep.

Then he laid his arm around the thin shoulders of the Jew and said softly:

'Sleep, dear Jew. Have a good sleep!'

He stayed awake a long time. Mendel Singer slept and snored. The frogs croaked until morning.

VIII

Two weeks later a small two-wheeled wagon rolled before Mendel Singer's house in a great cloud of dust, and brought a guest: it was Kapturak.

He announced that the papers were ready. Should an answer come within four weeks from Shemariah, called Sam, the journey of the Singer family would be certain. That was all Kapturak had to say, and that an advance of twenty roubles would be more satisfactory to him than having to deduct the sum later, from what Shemariah would send.

Deborah went into the storeroom, built of decayed wooden boards in the courtyard, pulled her blouse over her head, drew a knotted handkerchief from her bosom, and counted eight hard roubles into her hand. Then she turned down her blouse again, went into the house, and said to Kapturak:

'This is all that I have been able to raise among the neighbours. You'll have to be content with it.'

'One makes allowances for an old customer,' said Kapturak, swung himself up on his little yellow feather-weight wagon, and disappeared as quickly as he had come, in a cloud of dust.

'Kapturak was at Mendel Singer's,' cried the people in the little town. 'Mendel is going to America.'

Actually, Mendel Singer's journey to America had already begun. Everybody gave him advice against sea-sickness. A few buyers came to look at Mendel's house. They were prepared to pay a thousand roubles for it, a sum for which Deborah would have given five years of her life.

But Mendel Singer said, 'Do you realize, Deborah, that Menuchim must stay behind? With whom will he stay? Next month Billes marries his daughter to Fogl, the musician. Until they have a child of their own, they can keep Menuchim. And for that we will give them the house and take no money.'

'Is it settled as far as you are concerned that Menuchim stays behind? There are still a few weeks, at least, before we leave, and in this time God might make a miracle.'

'If God makes a miracle, He won't announce it in advance,' answered Mendel. 'One must hope. If we don't go to America, there will be a misfortune with Miriam. If we go to America, we must leave Menuchim behind. Shall we send Miriam to America by herself? Who knows what she would do, alone on the journey, and alone in America! Menuchim is so sick that only a miracle can help him. If a miracle helps him, he can follow us. Because although America is a long way off, it is still in this world.'

Deborah was silent. She heard the words of the Rabbi of Kluczysk: 'Do not leave him, stay with him, as though he were a healthy child.' She was not staying with him. For long years, day and night, hour after hour, she had waited for the promised miracle. The dead, beyond, did not help; the Rabbi did not help; God did not want to help. She had wept an ocean of tears. Night had been in her heart, misery in every pleasure, since the day of Menuchim's birth. All festivals had been tortures, and all holidays had been days of mourning. There was no spring and no summer. All seasons were winter. The sun rose, but it did not warm. Hope alone refused to die. 'He will always be a cripple,' said the neighbours. For they had not been visited with misfortune, and he who has had no misfortunes does not believe in miracles.

Yes, and those who have misfortunes do not believe in miracles. Miracles happened long, long ago, when the Jews still lived in Palestine. Since then there have been no more. And yet – hadn't people told of many miraculous deeds of the Rabbi of Kluczysk? The Rabbi had looked at her, had said his say, had spat three times. And Piczenik's daughter had gone away whole, light-hearted and clear-headed.

Other folk have luck, thought Deborah. For miracles

to happen one has to have luck. But Mendel Singer's children had no luck! They were just a teacher's children!

'If you were clever,' she said to Mendel, 'you would go to Kluczysk tomorrow, and ask the Rabbi's advice.'

'I?' asked Mendel. 'I should go to the Rabbi? You were there once. Go again. You believe in him; he would give you advice. You know that I don't believe in that sort of thing. No Jew needs a mediator between himself and God. He hears our prayers if we are righteous. When we sin, though, He can punish us.'

'Why does He punish us now? Have we sinned? Why is He so cruel?'

'You blaspheme Him, Deborah. Leave me in peace – I cannot talk with you any longer.' And Mendel Singer buried himself in a pious book.

Deborah caught up her shawl and went out. Outside stood Miriam. She stood there, rosy from the setting sun, with her smooth, shining black hair, wearing a white dress that now shimmered an orange colour. She was gazing straight into the sunset with her great black eyes, which she held wide open, although it seemed the sun would blind them.

'She is beautiful,' thought Deborah. 'I was as beautiful as that once – as beautiful as my daughter. And what has become of me? I have become Mendel Singer's wife. Miriam goes with a Cossack; she is beautiful – perhaps she is right.'

Miriam seemed not to see her mother. She observed with passionate intensity the glowing sun, which was now settling behind a violet wall of cloud. For several days this dark mass had appeared every evening, had prophesied storm and rain, and had disappeared next day. Miriam had noticed that, at the moment when the sun finally sank, over there in the cavalry barracks the soldiers would begin to sing; the whole company would sing, and always the same song: *polubyl ya tibia za tvoyu krasatu*. The day's work was finished; the Cossacks greeted the evening.

Miriam hummed the text of the song, of which she only knew the first two verses: I have fallen in love with you, because of your beauty. A whole company sang this song to her! A hundred men sang to her! In an hour she would meet one of them, or maybe two. Sometimes, even, three came.

She caught sight of her mother and remained standing quiet. She knew that Deborah would come over to her. For weeks the mother had not dared to call Miriam to her. It was as though Miriam exhaled the terror which surrounded the Cossacks, as though she was already under the protection of the strange, wild barracks.

No, Deborah no longer called Miriam. Deborah came to Miriam. Deborah, in an old shawl, stood there, old, ugly, nervous, before the gilded Miriam, holding the rail of the wooden pavement, as though she followed an old law which commanded an ugly mother to stand below a beautiful daughter.

'Your father is angry, Miriam,' said Deborah.

'Let him be angry,' said Miriam. 'Your Mendel Singer!'

For the first time Deborah heard the father's name

from the mouth of one of her children. For a moment it seemed to her that a stranger spoke, not Mendel's child. A stranger – why should she say 'Father'. Deborah wanted to turn away; she had made a mistake; she had spoken to a stranger. She did half-turn.

'Wait!' said Miriam, and Deborah felt, for the first time, how hard her daughter's voice was. 'A copper voice,' thought Deborah. It sounded like one of the church bells which she hated and feared.

'Stay here, Mother,' repeated Miriam. 'Let him alone, that man! Go with me to America! Leave Mendel Singer and Menuchim, the idiot, here!'

'I begged him to go to the Rabbi, and he won't. I won't go alone again to Kluczysk. I'm afraid. He has forbidden me once to leave Menuchim, even if his illness should last for years. What could I say to him, Miriam? Shall I tell him that we go to America because you – because you—'

'Because I run around with Cossacks,' finished Miriam, without moving. And she continued: 'Tell him what you will; it's none of my business. In America, I'll be even better able to do as I please. Because you married a Mendel Singer, do I have to marry one? Maybe you have a better husband for me? Have you a dowry for your daughter?'

Miriam did not raise her voice, and her questions did not sound like questions; it was as though she spoke of everyday things, as though she gave information about the price of greens and eggs. 'She's right,' thought Deborah. 'God help us, she's right!'

Deborah called upon all the good spirits to help her. For she felt that her daughter was right; she herself spoke out of the mouth of her daughter. And she began to fear herself, as a moment before she had feared Miriam. Threatening things were happening. The song of the soldiers drifted over, continually. The little strip of red sun still shone over the violet.

'I must go,' said Miriam, and drew away from the wall against which she had been leaning, fluttered light as a white butterfly from the pavement, walked with quick, coquettish feet, in the middle of the street, out in the direction of the barracks, towards the beckoning song of the Cossacks.

Fifty paces from the barracks, in the middle of a little path between the great forest and Sameshkin's fields, she waited for Ivan.

'We are going to America,' said Miriam.

'You won't forget me,' begged Ivan. 'Always, at this time, when the sun goes down, think of me and not of the others. And perhaps, with God's help, I'll come after you. You must write. Pavel will read me your letters; don't write about our secrets, or I'll be ashamed.'

He kissed Miriam, warmly, and many times. His kisses resounded like shots through the evening. A devil of a girl, he thought; now she goes off to America, and I shall have to find me another. There isn't another one about here as beautiful as she, and I have four years still to serve. He was huge, strong as a bear, and shy. His great hands trembled when he went to touch a girl. And he had not been at home in love.

Miriam had taught him all he knew. And what ideas she had had!

They embraced, as they had done yesterday, and the day before, in the middle of the field, bedded amidst the fruits of the earth, surrounded and shaded by the vaulted arch of the wheat. The ears of grain lay down willingly when Miriam and Ivan sank upon them; before the two sank on them, the ears seemed to lay themselves down. Today their love was shorter, more passionate, and at the same time anxious. It was as though Miriam must go to America tomorrow. The farewell already trembled in their love-making. Even while they grew into each other, they were far apart, separated by an ocean.

'How good,' thought Miriam, 'that I am going away and not he; that it's not I who'll be left behind!'

They lay for a long time, exhausted, helpless, speechless, as though sorely wounded. A thousand thoughts went to and fro in their brains. They did not notice the rain, which had come at last. It began softly and craftily; it was a long time before the drops were heavy enough to break through the thick golden enclosure of the ears. Suddenly they were at the mercy of the streaming water. They awakened, and began to run. The rain confused them, changed the world completely, took away their sense of time. They thought it must already be late; they listened for the sound of the bells in the tower, but only the rain roared, louder, faster, stilling mysteriously all the other sounds of the night. They kissed each other on their wet faces, pressed each other's hands. Water was between them; neither could feel the body of the other.

They took leave of each other hastily; their ways parted; already Ivan was enveloped and invisible in the rain.

'I shall never see him again,' thought Miriam, as she ran home. 'The harvest is here. Tomorrow the peasants will be scared, because one rain brings others.'

She reached home, and waited awhile under the shelter of the eaves, as though it were possible to become dry in a moment. She resolved to enter the room. It was dark. They were all asleep. She lay down quietly, wet as she was, let her clothes dry on her body, and did not stir again. Outside, the rain poured down.

Everybody knew now that Mendel was going to America. One pupil after another absented himself from instruction. There were only five boys left, and they came irregularly. Kapturak had not yet brought their papers; Sam had not yet sent the steamship tickets. But the house of Mendel Singer began to collapse.

'How rotten it must have been,' thought Mendel Singer. 'It was rotten, and we had not noticed it. He who does not give heed is like a deaf man, but is worse off than a deaf man – so it is written somewhere or other. My father was teacher here, and my grandfather; and here I, too, was a teacher. Now I am going to America. The Cossacks have taken my son Jonas, and they want to take Miriam from me also. Menuchim – what will become of Menuchim?'

On the evening of this same day he paid a visit to the Billes family. It was a happy family. It seemed to Mendel Singer as though they had a lot of unearned luck. All the daughters were married, even to the youngest, to whom he himself was going to offer his house; all three sons had escaped military service and had gone out into the world, one to Hamburg, another to California, the third to Paris. It was a happy family, God's hand rested over them; they lay snugly at peace in God's broad hand.

Old Billes was always gay. Mendel Singer had taught all of his sons. Old Billes had been a student of old Singer. Because they had known each other so long, Mendel Singer felt that he had some small claim upon their good fortune.

Mendel Singer's proposition pleased the Billes family. They were not too well off. Good! The young couple would take the house, and Menuchim with it.

'He won't give you any trouble,' said Mendel Singer. 'Each year he improves a little. Soon, with God's help, he will be quite well. Then my older son, Shemariah, will come over and get him, or he will send someone to bring Menuchim to America.'

'And what do you hear from Jonas?' asked old Billes.

For a long time now Mendel had heard nothing from his Cossack, as he called his son in secret – not without contempt, nor yet without pride. But he answered, 'Nothing but what's good! He has learned to read and write, and he has been promoted. Who knows, if he were not a Jew, he might already be an officer!' For it was impossible for Mendel Singer, in the face of this lucky family, to stand there with the crushing burden of his misfortunes upon his back. So he squared his shoulders and lied himself a little happiness.

It was fixed that Mendel Singer should turn the use of

his house over to the Billes family before simple witnesses, and avoid all official measures, which would cost money. Three or four respectable Jews would be sufficient as witnesses. In the meantime, Mendel received an advance of thirty roubles, because his students had ceased to come, and money was still going out.

A week later Kapturak rolled up again in his light yellow wagon. Everything had come: money, steamship tickets, passports, visas, the head tax for each, and even the fee for Kapturak.

'A punctual payer,' said Kapturak. 'Your son Shemariah, called Sam, is a punctual payer. A gentleman, as they say over there.'

Kapturak intended to accompany the Singer family to the border. In four weeks the steamship *Neptune* was sailing from Bremen to New York.

The Billes family came to take an inventory. Deborah was taking with her the bedding, six pillows, six sheets, and six red-and-blue checked quilts. The straw mattresses and Menuchim's poor bedding would remain.

Although Deborah had little to pack, and although every stick and stitch of her possessions was listed in her head, she was eternally busy. She packed; she unpacked. She counted the dishes, and then counted them once again. Menuchim broke two plates. He seemed all of a sudden to abandon his stupid inactivity. He called his mother oftener than usual. The single word that he had been able to speak all these years was repeated a dozen times even when his mother was nowhere around.

He was an idiot, this Menuchim. An idiot! How easily

one said that! But who could say what storms of terror and misery Menuchim's soul had to bear in these days – Menuchim's soul, which God had buried in the impenetrable fastnesses of his feeble mind! Yes, he was frightened, the cripple, Menuchim! He sometimes crept by himself out of his corner to the door, where he squatted on the sill in the sun like a sick dog, and blinked at the passersby, seeming to see only their boots, their trousers, their stockings, and their coats. Sometimes he would pull suddenly at his mother's apron, and whimper. Deborah would take him in her arms, although he was heavy.

Nevertheless, she held him in her arms, and sang two or three broken snatches of a lullaby that she herself had already forgotten, but that began to awaken in her memory whenever she held her unfortunate son in her arms. Then she set him down again, and went back to her work, which for days had consisted of packing and counting.

She stood still for a moment with meditative eyes. They were not unlike Menuchim's; so without life were they, so helplessly seeking in the unknown distance for the thoughts which her brain refused to deliver. Her distrait glance fell upon the sack into which she was going to sew the pillows, and it occurred to her: 'Couldn't we sew Menuchim into a sack?' Immediately she trembled, imagining that the customs officials might stick spears through the passengers' sacks. And she began to unpack, resolved to stay, and to follow the words of the Rabbi of Kluczysk: 'Do not leave your son; he is yours even as a healthy child is.' But the strength which belongs with faith was no longer hers, and gradually she was also losing the strength which is needed to endure despair.

It was as though they – Deborah and Mendel – had not voluntarily made the decision to go to America, but as though America had overcome them, had beset them, with Shemariah, Mac, and Kapturak. They could no longer save themselves from America. The documents came to them, the steamship tickets, the head taxes.

'How would it be,' asked Deborah, 'if Menuchim should suddenly become well – today, or tomorrow?'

Mendel shook his head. Then he said: 'If Menuchim becomes well, we take him with us!' And both of them indulged silently in the hope that Menuchim would rise from his bed tomorrow or the day after, strong and well, with sound limbs and a complete vocabulary.

They were to start on Sunday. It was Thursday. For the last time Deborah stood before her stove to prepare the Sabbath meal, the white poppy-seed bread, the braided hard rolls. The fire burned, hissed, and crackled, and smoke filled the room, as it had on every Thursday for thirty years. Outside it was raining. The rain in the chimney drove the smoke back into the room; the old, familiar jagged dent in the ceiling plaster displayed itself again in its fresh dampness. For ten years the hole in the roof's shingles should have been repaired; the Billes family would do it. The great iron-bound brown trunks stood ready packed, with strong iron rods across the openings, and with two brand-new gleaming iron locks.

Sometimes Menuchim crept about them and pounded them with his fists. Then there was an unholy rattling; the locks smote against the iron bands, and trembled, and would not stop. And the fire crackled, and smoke filled the room.

On the evening before the Sabbath, Mendel Singer took leave of his neighbours. They drank a yellowish-green brandy which one of them had himself brewed and mixed with dried mushrooms. Thus the brandy was not only sharp but bitter. The farewell took more than an hour. Everyone wished Mendel luck. Some looked at him doubtfully; some envied him. But all said that America was a wonderful country. A Jew could wish for nothing better than to get to America.

During this night Deborah left her bed and, shielding a candle carefully with her hand, went to Menuchim's pallet. He lay on his back, his heavy head resting on a rolled-up grey blanket, his lids half open, so that one saw the whites of his eyes. At each breath his body trembled; his sleeping fingers moved constantly. He held his hands on his breast. In sleep his face was even more sallow and flabby than it was by day. The blue lips stood open; white drops of foam gathered in the corners of his mouth. Deborah put out the light. She crouched for a few moments beside her son, rose, and crept back into bed. He will amount to nothing, she thought. He will amount to nothing. She did not sleep any more.

On Sunday at eight o'clock in the morning, a messenger came from Kapturak. It was the man with the blue cap, the same fellow who had taken Shemariah over the frontier. Today, also, the man with the blue cap stood outside the door, refused the tea which was offered him, silently helped to roll out the trunks and put them on the wagon. A comfortable wagon. Place for four persons. Their feet rested in soft hay; the wagon smelled like the whole land in late summer. The backs of the horses gleamed, brushed and shining, convex brown mirrors. A wide yoke, with many little silver bells, was across their proud and slender necks. Although it was bright daylight, one saw the shower of sparks which their hoofs beat from the stones of the road.

Once again Deborah held Menuchim in her arms. The Billes family were already there; they surrounded the wagon and talked continually. Mendel Singer sat next to the driver, and Miriam leaned her back against her father's. Only Deborah still stood before the door, with the cripple Menuchim in her arms.

Suddenly she left him. She laid him gently down upon the doorsill as one lays a corpse in a coffin, stood up, stretched herself erect, and let her tears flow. Naked tears over her naked face. She had made up her mind. Her son was to stay. She would go to America. There had been no miracle.

Weeping, she climbed into the wagon. She did not see the faces of the people whose hands she pressed. Her two eyes were two great oceans of tears. She heard the clatter of the horses' hoofs. She was off.

She cried aloud; she did not know that she cried aloud; something cried in her; her heart had a mouth and cried. The wagon stopped; she leapt out of it, as light-footed as a boy. Menuchim still sat on the doorsill. She fell on her knees before him. Mama! Mama! babbled Menuchim. She could not rise.

The Billes family lifted Deborah. She screamed; she thrust them off; finally she was quiet. They helped her to the wagon and laid her in the hay. The wagon rolled quickly towards Dubno.

Six hours later they sat in the railway carriage in the slow train, together with many unknown people. The train journeyed gently through the land; the fields and meadows where the harvest was being gathered, the peasants and the peasant women, the herds and the huts seemed to be greeting the train. The sleepy song of the wheels lulled the passengers. Deborah had not spoken a word. She slumbered. The wheels of the train repeated endlessly, endlessly: Do not leave him! Do not leave him!

Mendel Singer prayed. He knew his prayers by heart; he prayed mechanically. He did not think of the meaning of the words; their sound alone was sufficient; God understood what they meant. Thus Mendel Singer deadened his great fear of the water, on which he soon would be. Sometimes he cast an absent-minded glance at Miriam. She sat opposite him, beside the man with the blue cap. Mendel did not see how she snuggled close to the man. The man did not speak to her; he waited for the short quarter of an hour between the time when twilight would descend and when the conductor would light the gas lamps. The man with the cap was promising himself all sorts of delights in this quarter of an hour – and later, in the night, when the gas flame would be put out.

Next morning he took leave of the older Singers indifferently. But he pressed Miriam's hand with silent warmth. They had reached the border. The border control took their passports. When they called Mendel's name he trembled. Without any reason. Everything was in order. They were passed.

They climbed into the next train, saw more stations, heard new signals, saw new uniforms. They travelled for three days, and changed once. On the afternoon of the third day they arrived in Bremen. A man from the steamship company bellowed: Mendel Singer! The Singer family revealed themselves. The official awaited no less than nine families. He stood them in a row, counted them three times, called out their names, and gave each a number. Now they stood there, with no idea what to do with the lead checks. He had promised to come back soon. But the nine families – twenty-five persons – did not move. They stood in a row on the railway platform, the checks in their hands, their bundles at their feet. At the farthest corner, to the left, because he had announced himself so late, stood Mendel Singer.

During the entire journey he had hardly exchanged a word with his wife and daughter. Both women had been dumb. But now Deborah seemed unable to endure her silence any longer.

'Why don't you move?' asked Deborah.

'No one is moving,' answered Mendel.

'Why don't you ask the people around what we should do?'

'No one is asking.'

'What are we waiting for?'

'I don't know why we are waiting.'

'Do you think I might sit on my bag?'

'Sit on your bag.'

In the very moment, however, when Deborah had spread her skirts to sit down, the official from the steamship company appeared and announced in Russian, Polish, German, and Yiddish that he now planned to accompany all nine families to the harbour; that he would settle them in a barracks there for the night; and that the next day, at seven in the morning, the *Neptune* would lift anchor.

They slept in the barracks, in Bremerhaven, the checks clasped tightly in their fists, even while they slumbered. The balcony trembled and the little yellow electric bulbs swung softly to and fro from the snoring of the twenty-five, and from their constant turning on the hard pallets. It was forbidden to make tea. They had gone to sleep with dry mouths. But a Polish barber had offered Miriam red bon-bons. Miriam went to sleep with a great sticky candy-drop in her mouth.

Mendel awoke at five o'clock in the morning. He climbed out of his wooden bunk with difficulty, looked for the water faucet, went out to see in which direction lay the east. Then he returned, stood in a corner, and prayed. He whispered his prayer, but while he whispered, such intense pain attacked him, clawing and tearing violently at his heart, that he groaned aloud. A few sleepers awakened, looked down, and grinned at the Jew, who hopped and swayed in the corner, rocking

111

his body backwards and forwards, in a miserable dance to the glory of God.

Mendel had not yet finished when the official pulled open the door. A sea wind seemed to have blown him into the barracks.

'Everybody up!' he cried several times, in all the languages of the world.

It was still early when they reached the ship. They were allowed to peep a few times into the dining-rooms of the first and second class, before they were pushed between decks. Mendel Singer did not move. He stood on the top step of a narrow iron ladder. At his back was the harbour, the land, the continent, his home, the past. At his left beamed the sun. The sky was blue. The ship was white. The water was green. A sailor came and ordered Mendel Singer to leave the stairs. He dismissed the sailor with a gesture. He was entirely calm, and without fear. He cast a fleeting glance at the ocean, and drank solace from the infinitude of the moving waters. The ocean was eternal. Mendel knew that God Himself had created it. He had poured it out from His inexhaustible fountains. Now it rocked to and fro between the lands of the earth. Deep down, at the bottom of the sea, Leviathan lay curled, the holy fish, whom the pious and the righteous would eat on the Day of Judgment. The ship on which Mendel stood was called *Neptune*. It was a great ship. But compared with Leviathan, with the ocean, with the heavens, and with the wisdom of the Eternal, it was a tiny ship. No, Mendel felt no anxiety. He quieted the sailor, he, a little black Jew on an enormous ship, before the eternal ocean. He turned again, describing a semicircle, and murmuring the blessing which is to be said at the first sight of the sea. He turned, in a half-circle, and strewed the isolated words of the blessing over the green surging: 'Praised art thou, eternal One, our God, who hast created the ocean and with it hast divided the continents!'

At this moment the siren sounded. The engines began to rumble. And air, and ship, and men all trembled. Only the sky remained blue and silent, silent and blue.

IX

THE FOURTEENTH NIGHT of the journey was lighted by great round fiery spheres discharged by the light-ships.

'Now,' said a Jew who had made the trip twice to Mendel Singer, 'we shall see the Statue of Liberty. She is a hundred and fifty feet high, is hollow in the centre, and you can climb up in her. Around her head she wears a crown of light. In her right hand she holds a torch. And the best of all is that this torch burns in the night, and yet is never burnt up. Because it's only electric light. That's the kind of trick that they can do in America!'

They disembarked on the fifteenth day. Deborah, Miriam, and Mendel stood close together, because they were afraid of losing each other. Men in uniform appeared. They seemed a little dangerous to Mendel, although they carried no sabres. A few wore clothes as white as blossoms, and looked somewhat like gendarmes and somewhat like angels. Those must be the American Cossacks, thought Mendel, and watched his daughter Miriam.

They were called according to the alphabet. Each arrived at his luggage; no one pierced it with sharp spears. Perhaps we could have brought Menuchim along, thought Deborah.

Suddenly Shemariah stood before them.

All three of them started, in the same fashion.

All three of them saw, simultaneously, their little old house, the old Shemariah, and the new Shemariah, called Sam.

They saw Shemariah and Sam at the same time; as though Sam were superimposed on Shemariah, a transparent Sam.

To be sure it was Shemariah, but it was also Sam.

There were two of them. The one wore a black cap, a black robe, and high boots, and the first downy black hairs sprouted from the pores of his cheeks.

The second wore a light grey coat, a snow-white cap, like that of the captain, wide yellow trousers, a brilliant shirt of green silk, and his countenance was as smooth as an elegant gravestone.

The second was almost Mac.

The first spoke with his old voice; they heard the voice, not the words.

The second slapped his father on the shoulder with a

heavy hand, and said – and now they heard the words: 'Hello, old man!' But they understood nothing.

The first was Shemariah. The second, though, was Sam.

First, Sam kissed his father, then his mother, then Miriam. All three sniffed Sam's shaving soap, which smelled a little like the lilies-of-the-valley from the woods at home, and a little like carbolic acid. Sam reminded them at once of a garden and a hospital.

Silently, they repeated to themselves that Sam was Shemariah. Then, at length, they were glad.

'All the others,' said Sam, 'have to go through quarantine. Not you! Mac fixed it. He has two cousins working here.'

Half an hour later Mac appeared.

He looked exactly as he had before, when he appeared in the little town; broad-shouldered, loud-voiced, rumbling forth an unintelligible language, his pockets swollen with cookies which he immediately distributed and which he himself began to munch. A screaming red tie flapped over his breast like a flag.

'You've got to go through quarantine after all,' said Mac. For, it came out, Mac had exaggerated. To be sure he had two cousins in the service, but they were only in the customs department. 'But I'll go with you. Don't worry.'

They really had no need to worry. Mac yelled at all the officials that Miriam was his betrothed, and Mendel and Deborah his parents-in-law.

Every afternoon at three o'clock, Mac came to visit

them. He stuck a hand through the wire, although this was prohibited, and greeted everyone. After four days he succeeded in freeing the Singer family. How he managed it, he did not divulge. For it was characteristic of Mac that he would brag with enthusiasm of things which were total fabrications, and remain entirely silent about things which he really accomplished.

He insisted that they must see America thoroughly – from an open wagon belonging to his firm – before they went home. He invited Mendel Singer, Deborah, and Miriam, and showed them the sights.

It was a clear, hot day. Mendel and Deborah sat facing the front. Miriam sat opposite them. The heavy wagon rattled through the streets with angry momentum. It seemed to Mendel Singer as though the wagon intended to crush the stone and asphalt of the street for ever, and shake the houses to their foundations. The leather seats burned under Mendel Singer's body like a hot oven. Although they kept in the dark shadows of the high buildings, the heat burned like melted lead through the old cap of black silk rep which Mendel wore on his skull, penetrated into his brain, and soldered it up, with a damp, sticky, painful glow. Since his arrival he had not slept, had hardly eaten, and had drunk almost nothing. He wore his native galoshes of rubber over his heavy shoes, and his feet burned as in an open fire. He held his umbrella cramped between his knees. Its wooden handle was as hot as red iron. Before Mendel's eyes floated a thick veil of soot, dust, and heat. He thought of the desert through which his ancestors had wandered forty years. But they, at least, went on foot, he said to himself. The mad haste in which they now travelled created, to be sure, a wind, but it was a hot wind, the fiery breath of hell. Instead of being cool, it glowed. The wind was no wind; it was shouting and alarm; it was a floating noise. In it were the shrill ringing of hundreds of invisible bells; the dangerous metallic thunder of trains; the tooting of countless horns; the beseeching scream of the tracks at the curves of the streets; the roaring of Mac; the murmur of the people around Mendel; the raucous laughter of someone sitting at his back; the unintermittent talk which Sam hurled into his father's face, which Mendel did not understand, but which he answered constantly by a nod, a fearful and yet friendly smile fixed on his lips as though clamped there with iron.

Even if he had had the courage to maintain an earnest mien, as befitted his station, he could not have stopped smiling. He did not have the strength to change his expression. The muscles of his face were paralysed. He could rather have wept, like a small child. He smelled the sharp tar odour of the melting asphalt; the dry, parched dust in the air; the rancid and greasy stink of the river and the cheese shops; the mordant smell of onions; the sweetish gasolene fumes of automobiles; the foul, swampy smell of fish markets; and the carbolic acid and lilies-of-the-valley on the cheeks of his son.

All the smells united in a hot vapour, together with the noise which filled his ears and threatened to split his skull. Soon he no longer knew whether he was hearing, seeing, smelling. He went on smiling and nodding. America pressed down on him; America broke him; America shattered him. After a few minutes he became unconscious.

He awakened in a lunchroom, where they had brought him in haste, to bathe his face. In a round mirror, wreathed with a hundred little glowing electric bulbs, he glimpsed his white beard and his bony nose, and believed, for a moment, that nose and beard belonged to someone else. He recognized himself only when he saw his family standing about him. He was embarrassed. With difficulty he opened his lips and begged his son's pardon. Mac grasped his hand and shook it, as though he congratulated Mendel on a successful trick or on a bet he had won. The iron clamp of the smile again settled around Mendel's lips, and the unknown power again moved his head so that it seemed as though Mendel nodded. He saw Miriam. Her black hair was disarranged under her yellow shawl, and there was soot on her pale cheeks. Deborah crouched, broad and silent, with distended nostrils and a bosom which rose and fell, on a round stool without a back, and looked as though she would fall any moment.

'What are these people to me!' thought Mendel Singer. 'What is all of America to me? My son, my daughter, my wife, this Mac? Am I still Mendel Singer? Is this still my family? Where is my son, Menuchim?'

It was as though he had been cast out of himself, separated from himself, and doomed to live on. It was as though he had left himself behind, in Zuchnow, near

Menuchim. And while his lips smiled, and his head nodded, his heart began slowly to freeze. It pounded like a metal drum-stick against cold glass. Already he was alone, was Mendel Singer. Already he was in America ...

Part Two

X

A FEW HUNDRED years earlier, an ancestor of Mendel Singer had probably gone from Spain to Volhynia. He had a luckier, more ordinary fate than that of his descendant; in any case, no one recorded it, and therefore we do not know whether it took him many years or few to become naturalized in a strange land. But of Mendel Singer we know that in a few months he was quite at home in New York.

Yes, he was almost a native of America! He already knew that 'old man' meant father and 'old lady' mother, or vice versa. He knew a few tradesmen from the Bowery who came to see his son; he knew Essex Street, where he lived, and Houston Street, where was his son's place of business – his son Sam. He knew that Sam was already an 'American fellow'; that, if one was a refined gentleman, one said 'Good-bye', 'How-do-you-do', and 'Please'; that a Grand Street merchant could command respect and might even live on Riverside Drive; and that Sam himself was beginning to think of that address, for himself.

They had told him that America was 'God's own country', as Palestine had once been; that New York was veritably a 'wonder city', a town of miracles, as Jerusalem had once been. Praying, however, was called 'service', and so were good deeds. Sam's small son, born barely a week after the arrival of his grandfather, was called nothing less than Mac Lincoln, and – for time passes quickly in America – would be a 'college boy' soon. The daughter-in-law already called the little one 'my dear boy'.

Incredible to believe, she herself was still called Vega! She was blonde and gentle, with blue eyes which seemed to Mendel Singer to reflect more goodness than cleverness. Let her be stupid! Women need no brains. God bless her. Amen.

Between twelve and two, one eats 'lunch'; between six and eight, 'dinner.' But Mendel did not observe these hours. He ate at three in the afternoon, and at ten at night, as at home, although, to be sure, it must still be daylight at home when he sat down to his evening meal, or even, perhaps, early morning. Who knows! 'All right' meant 'I agree'; and instead of 'Ja' one said 'Yes'. If one wished another well, one did not wish him health and happiness, but prosperity. In the immediate future Sam contemplated an apartment on the Drive, with a parlour. He already possessed a phonograph; Miriam borrowed it occasionally and carried it tenderly through the streets, as though it were a sick child. The phonograph could play many waltzes, but it also could play Kol-Nidre.

Sam washed twice a day, and the suit he often wore in the evening he called 'dress'. Deborah had already been ten times to the moving pictures and three times to the theatre. She had a dark-grey silk dress. Sam had given it to her. She wore a great golden chain around her neck; she reminded one of the Babylonish women, of whom the Scriptures told. Miriam was a saleslady in Sam's store. She came home at midnight, and left at seven in the morning. She said: 'Good evening, Father,' and 'Good morning, Father.' And apart from this, nothing at all.

Now and then Mendel Singer heard from the talk around him – it flowed past his ears as a river flows past the feet of an old man who stands on its banks – that Miriam went walking with Mac, that she danced with him, went swimming with him, went to the theatre with him. Mendel Singer knew that Mac was no Jew. The Cossacks were also not Jews; this affair had not gone so far; God will help; we shall see. Deborah and Miriam were getting on well together. There was peace in the house. The mother and daughter whispered together, late, after midnight. Mendel pretended to sleep.

He could pretend easily. He slept in the kitchen; mother and daughter slept in the single living-room. One did not dwell in palaces, even in America! But at least they lived on the first floor. What luck! How easily they might have had to live on the second, third, or fourth! The stairs were steep and dirty, and always dark. Even during the day one had to strike matches to see the way. It smelled warm, damp, and clammy, and it smelled of cats. And yet one had to mix rat poison and ground glass with dough, and put it in the corners every night. Deborah scrubbed the floor every week, but it was never so saffron-yellow as it had been at home. What was the reason? Had Deborah become weak? Was she lazy? Was she old?

All the boards squeaked when Mendel walked through the room. Now it was impossible to guess where Deborah hid her money. Sam gave ten dollars a week. Nevertheless Deborah was indignant. She was a woman; sometimes she seemed possessed. She had a kind, gentle daughter-in-law. But Deborah maintained that Vega indulged in luxuries. When Mendel heard this sort of talk he said:

'Keep still, Deborah! Be satisfied with the children! Aren't you old enough yet to have learned to hold your tongue! Is it that you can't complain any more that I don't earn enough; does it make you miserable that you can't quarrel with me any more? Shemariah has brought us here, so that we can grow old and die near to him. His wife honours us both, as she should. What more do you want, Deborah?'

She did not really know what she wanted. Perhaps she had hoped to find a completely new world in America, in which it would be possible to forget the old life, and Menuchim. But this America was no new world. There were more Jews here than in Kluczysk; it was really a larger Kluczysk. Had one made a vast journey over the wide ocean only to arrive again in Kluczysk, which one could reach with Sameshkin's wagon? The windows opened into a dark court in which cats, rats, and children romped and scuffled. At three in the afternoon, even in the springtime, you had to turn on the gaslight – and there was not even electric light, and they did not even have their own phonograph. At home Deborah had at least had light and sunshine. To be sure, she went now and then with her daughter-in-law to the movies; twice she had ridden in the subway; Miriam was an elegant young lady, with stockings and a hat. She had become very good. And she earned money, too. Mac went around with her. Better Mac than the Cossacks. He was Shemariah's best friend. One couldn't understand a word of his eternal talking, but one would get used to it. He was smarter than ten Jews, and he had this advantage, that he wouldn't ask for a dowry. After all, it was another world. Mac was no Russian Mac. An American Mac was not a Russian Mac.

Of course, you couldn't get along here, either, with the money you had. The cost of living went up visibly; Deborah could not give up saving. The usual floor-board already hid eighteen and a half dollars. The carrots diminished, the eggs were hollow, the potatoes froze, the soup was watery, the carp thin, the pike short, the ducks lean, the geese tough, and the chickens amounted to nothing.

No, she did not really know what was lacking. Menuchim was lacking. She missed Menuchim.

127

Sometimes in sleep, or awake, or as she shopped, or in the moving pictures, or as she cleaned the rooms, or baked the bread, she heard him call. 'Mama! Mama!' he called. The only word which he had learned to speak he must, by now, have forgotten. She heard strange children cry Mama and the mothers replied. No mother on earth would willingly leave her child. They ought not to have come to America. But they could always go back!

'Mendel,' she said, sometimes. 'Shan't we go back, and see Menuchim?'

'And the money, and the journey, and how shall we live? Do you think Shemariah has so much? He is a good son, but he is no Vanderbilt. Probably it had to be. Wait, for the time being. We shall see Menuchim here yet, when he is well.'

And nevertheless the thought of returning stuck fast in Mendel Singer's mind, and never left him. Once, when he went to visit his son in his store (he sat in the office behind a glass door, and saw every customer come and go, and in silence blessed everyone who entered), Mendel said to Shemariah: 'What would you think if I went over to see him?'

Shemariah, called Sam, was an American fellow. He said, 'Father, that's impractical. If only we could bring Menuchim here, he'd get well, right off. American medicine is the best in the world. I just read it in the newspaper. They cure such diseases with injections, simply with injections! But since we can't bring him over here, poor Menuchim, why spend the money? I won't say that it's out of the question. But just now, when Mac and I are making big business plans and are short of money, we can't even discuss it. Wait a few weeks. Confidentially, Mac and I are speculating in real estate. We've had an old house in Delancy Street torn down. I tell you, Father, it costs almost as much to tear down as to build! But one can't complain. We're getting on. When I think how we started with insurance! Ups and downs! And now we have this business, you can almost say, this department store! Now the insurance agents come to me! I look at them, think to myself, I know that business, and throw them out! I throw them all out!'

Mendel Singer was not quite clear why Sam threw out all the agents and why he was so pleased about it. Sam felt this, and said, 'Will you have lunch with me, Father?' He acted as though he had forgotten that his father only ate at home; he gladly created the opportunity to emphasize how far removed he was from his native customs; he struck his brow, as though he were Mac, and said, 'But of course! I had forgotten! But you will eat a banana, Father.' And he ordered a banana brought for his father.

'About Miriam now,' he continued, in the midst of his meal. 'She is getting on. She's the prettiest girl in the shop. If she were working for strangers they would have offered her a job as model, long ago. But I don't want to see my sister showing off her figure in clothes that aren't her own. And Mac doesn't want it, either.'

He waited to see whether his father would say anything about Mac. But Mendel Singer was silent. He was not suspicious. He had hardly heard the last sentence.

He was filled with admiration for his children, especially for Shemariah. How clever he was, how quickly he thought, how fluently he spoke English, how he could press buttons, and call messenger boys! He was a 'boss'.

He went into the department for shirts and cravats, to see his daughter.

'Good morning, Father!' she called, in the midst of serving a customer. She respected him. It had been otherwise at home. Probably she didn't care for him. But it is not written: Love thy father and thy mother, but: Honour thy father and thy mother. He nodded to her, and went on. He went home.

He was comforted. He walked slowly, in the middle of the street, greeted neighbours, was pleased by the children. He still wore his cap of black silk rep, the half-length caftan, and the high boots. But the skirts of his coat no longer beat with the tact of hasty wings against his boot shafts. For in America, where everybody hurried, Mendel Singer had first learned to walk slowly.

Thus he wandered towards old age, from morning prayer to evening prayer, from breakfast to supper, from awakening to sleep. In the afternoon, at the hour when his pupils had been accustomed to come, he laid himself on the horsehair sofa, slept an hour, and dreamed of Menuchim. Then he read a little in the Yiddish newspaper. Afterwards he went into the shop of the Skovronnek family where phonographs, records, sheet music, and song texts were sold, played, and sung. All the older folk of the neighbourhood foregathered there. They talked politics, and told anecdotes about home. Sometimes, when it grew late, they would go into the living-room of the Skovronneks and rush through the evening prayer.

On the way back, which Mendel usually tried to prolong, he would imagine that at home a letter would be awaiting him. The letter would set forth clearly and positively, first, that Menuchim had become quite well and intelligent; second, that Jonas, because of some minor offence, had left the service and was coming to America.

Mendel Singer knew that this letter had not come. But at the same time he encouraged himself to believe in it, so that he would have a pleasure in entering his house. He would turn the knob with a lightly palpitating heart. But the moment that he caught sight of Deborah, all was over. The letter was not yet there. This would be an evening like every other.

One day, as he went home by a roundabout route, he caught sight of a half-grown youth who seemed, in the distance, to be familiar. The boy leaned against the entrance to a house and wept. Mendel heard a thin whimper; gentle as it was, it reached Mendel on the opposite side of the street. How well Mendel knew this sound! He stopped. He decided to approach the boy, to question him, to comfort him.

He started towards him. Suddenly the whimpering became louder. Mendel stopped in the middle of the street. In the evening shadows about the doorway where the boy crouched, he seemed to take on Menuchim's shape and bearing. Just so, on the doorsill of the house in Zuchnow, had Menuchim crouched and whimpered.

Mendel took a few more steps. Then the boy scurried into the house. The dark hall swallowed him.

Even more slowly than usual, Mendel wandered home.

It was not Deborah whom he saw first when he entered, but his son Sam. Mendel hesitated a moment on the doorsill. Although he was prepared for nothing except a pleasurable surprise, he suddenly was frightened; a misfortune might have occurred. Yes, his heart was so accustomed to misfortune that he always started with a shock, even after long preparation for good luck. What joyful surprise, he thought, can a man like me experience? Everything sudden is evil; the good creeps slowly.

But Shemariah's voice quieted him.

'Come in!' said Sam.

He drew his father by the hand into the room. Deborah had lighted two lamps. His daughter-in-law Vega, Miriam, and Mac were sitting at the table. The whole house seemed to Mendel to have changed. The two lamps – they were exactly the same – looked like twins, and they lighted the house less than they did each other. It was as though they laughed at each other, and the thought made Mendel gay.

'Sit down, Father,' said Sam.

He was not curious, Mendel. Already he was afraid that one of those American stories was coming, which all the world seemed to find funny, and which Mendel could find no pleasure in at all.

'What's going to happen?' he thought. 'They will have

given me a phonograph. Or they have decided to get married.'

He sat down carefully. Everyone was silent. Then Sam said – and it was as though he lighted a third lamp in the room – 'Father, we have earned fifteen thousand dollars at one stroke!'

Mendel arose, and shook hands with everyone. Finally he reached Mac. Mendel said to him: 'I thank you.' Sam immediately translated the three words into English. Mac arose and embraced Mendel. Then he began to speak. He did not cease thereafter. Apart from Mac no one spoke a word during the rest of the evening.

Deborah changed the sum into roubles, and it seemed that she never would be done with figuring. Vega thought about new furniture, and, in particular, about a piano. Her son ought to have piano lessons. Mendel thought of a trip home. Miriam only heard Mac talking, and did her best to understand him. Because she did not entirely understand what he said, she thought that Mac spoke too cleverly to be easily understood. Sam considered whether he ought to put the whole sum of money into his business. Only Mac thought little, if at all; he had no cares, built no plans. He said what came into his head.

The next day they went to Atlantic City. 'Nature here is beautiful,' said Deborah. Mendel saw only the water. And he remembered the wild night at home when he had lain with Sameshkin in the ditch by the side of the road. And he heard the chirp of the crickets and the croaking of the frogs.

'At home,' he said suddenly, 'the earth is as wide as the water is in America.' He had not wanted to say that at all.

'Did you hear what your father said?' commented Deborah. 'He's getting old.'

Yes, yes, I am getting old, thought Mendel.

When they reached home a thick, swollen letter was sticking out of the letter box. The postman had not been able to get it in.

'Look,' said Mendel. 'This letter is a good letter. Our luck has begun. One luck brings another, praise God. May He help us further.'

It was a letter from the Billes family. And it was indeed a good letter. It contained the news that Menuchim had suddenly begun to talk.

'Doctor Soltysiuk saw him,' wrote the Billes family. 'He couldn't believe it. They want to send Menuchim to Petersburg. The big doctors will rack their brains over him. One day, it was Thursday, he was home alone and there was a fire in the stove, like every Thursday. A burning stick fell out and now the whole floor is scorched and the walls, we had to tint them over. It cost a pretty penny, too. Menuchim ran into the street, he can walk quite well now, and cried, "It's burning." And since then he can speak a few words.

'Too bad, though, that it all happened a week after Jonas left. Because your Jonas was here, on a vacation, and he is really already a great soldier, and he didn't even know you were in America. And he is writing to you, too, on the other side.'

Mendel turned the page over and read:

'Dear Father, dear Mother, dear Brother, and dear Sister!

'So you are in America! It struck me like lightning. It's my own fault, of course, because I never, or I guess just once, wrote to you, just the same, as I say, it struck me like lightning. Don't worry though, I am fine. Everybody is good to me, and I get on with everyone. I am especially good with horses. I can ride like the best Cossack and pick a handkerchief off the ground with my teeth at full gallop. I like such things and I like the army too. I am going to stay here after my service term is up. They take care of you in the army, you get your food, the ones above tell you everything you have to do, you don't have to do any thinking yourself. I don't know whether I write it so that you can really understand what I mean. It's warm in the stalls, and I like the horses. If one of you should come over here you could see me. My captain says that if I stay such a good soldier I can petition the Tsar, I mean his noble and gracious Majesty, to pardon my brother's desertion. That would be my greatest joy, to see Shemariah again in this life; after all we grew up together.

'Sameshkin sends best wishes. He's fine.

'Here they say sometimes that there'll be a war. If it really should come you must be prepared for me to die, just as I'm prepared for it, because I'm a soldier.

'Just in case that should happen I embrace you all, once and for ever. But don't be sad. Perhaps I'll live.

'Your son Jonas.'

Mendel Singer laid aside his glasses, observed that Deborah wept, and for the first time in many long years, he grasped both her hands. He drew her hands away from her tear-stained countenance and said, almost solemnly:

'Well, Deborah, God has helped us. Take your shawl, run down and bring a bottle of mead.'

They sat at the table and drank the mead from tea glasses, gazed at each other, and thought the same thoughts.

'The Rabbi was right,' said Deborah. Her memory clearly dictated to her the words which had slumbered in it, for so long: 'Pain will make him wise, ugliness good, bitterness mild, and sickness strong.'

'You never told me that,' said Mendel.

'I had forgotten it.'

'You ought to have taken Jonas to Kluczysk, too. He loves his horses more than he does us.'

'He's still young,' comforted Deborah. 'Perhaps it's well that he loves horses.' And because she could never let an opportunity for malice pass, she added: 'He certainly doesn't get his love of horses from you.'

'No,' said Mendel, and smiled peaceably.

He began to think of returning home. Now, perhaps, one could soon bring Menuchim to America. He lighted a candle, extinguished the lamp, and said, 'Go to sleep, Deborah! When Miriam comes home I'll show her the letter. Tonight, I shall stay up.'

From his trunk, he fetched his old prayerbook, so familiar to his hand. He opened immediately to the Psalms, and sang one after the other. He had experienced grace and joy.

God's broad, wide, kindly hand arched protectingly over him, too. Sheltered by it, and in honour of it, he sang the Psalms, one after the other. The candle flickered in the gentle but fervent breeze kindled by Mendel's swaying body. With his feet he kept time to the rhythm of the Psalms. His heart rejoiced, and his body had to dance.

XI

Now care, for the first time, deserted the house of Mendel Singer. She had become familiar to him as a hated member of the family. He was now fifty-nine years old. And for fifty-eight years he had known care. Care left him; death approached. His beard was white; his eyes weak. His back was bent; his hands trembled. His sleep was light, and the nights were long. He wore contentment as a strange, borrowed garment.

His son moved into a wealthy neighbourhood. Mendel stayed in his alley, in his old flat, with the blue gas lamp, in the neighbourhood of the poor, the cats, and the mice. He was pious, God-fearing, and ordinary, an entirely commonplace Jew.

Few observed him; many people failed to notice him at all. By day he visited a few old friends: Menkes, who

138

kept a fruit shop; Skovronnek, who had the music store; Rottenberg, the Bible copyist; Groschel, the shoemaker. Once a week his three children visited him, with his grandchild and Mac. He had nothing to say to them. They spoke of the theatre, of society, of politics. He listened and dozed. When Deborah called him, he opened his eyes.

'I wasn't asleep,' he would assure them.

Mac laughed, Sam smiled. Miriam and Deborah whispered together. Mendel would stay awake awhile, and then nod again.

Immediately he would dream. He dreamt of events at home, and things which he had only heard about in America: theatres, acrobats and dancers in red and gold, the President of the United States, the White House, the millionaire Vanderbilt, and ever and ever again – Menuchim. The little cripple was mixed up with his dreams of prima donnas in red and gold; or he became a poor grey spot amidst the pale beams in which the White House stood. Mendel was too old to look at this or that with open eyes. He took his children's word for it, that America was God's country, New York a city of miracles, and English the most beautiful language in the world.

Americans were healthy, their women pretty, sport was important, time was money, poverty was a crime, riches a service, virtue was half of success, and belief in oneself the whole of it, dancing was hygienic, roller-skating a duty, charity was an investment, anarchism a crime, strikers were enemies of mankind, agitators instruments of the Devil, modern machinery a gift of God, Edison the world's greatest genius.

Soon men would fly like birds, swim like fishes, foresee the future like prophets, live in eternal peace and harmony, and build skyscrapers to touch the stars.

The world will be very beautiful, thought Mendel. How lucky my grandchild is! He will live through it all!

And, nevertheless, mixed with his admiration for the future was a nostalgia for Russia, and it calmed and comforted him to think that, before the living had their triumph, he would be dead. He did not know why he felt so. But it eased him. He was already too old for these new things, and too weak for triumph. But he had one hope left: to see Menuchim. Sam or Mac would go over and fetch him. Perhaps Deborah would go, too.

It was summer. The vermin in Mendel's flat reproduced themselves zealously, although the little metal wheels on the feet of the bed stood day and night in basins of kerosene, and although Deborah, with a feather dipped in turpentine, painted all the cracks in the furniture. The bedbugs marched down the walls in orderly ranks, went into formations on the ceiling, waited with bloodthirsty malice for the advent of darkness, and fell upon the camp of the sleepers. The cockroaches ran out of the cracks near the kitchen sink, among the dishes, into the food. The nights were hot and oppressive. Through the open window came, from time to time, the distant rumble of unknown trains, the short, regular thunder of miles of busy world, and the thick steam from neighbours' houses, from garbage cans and dirty gutters. Cats yowled, homeless dogs howled, infants shrieked through the night, and above Mendel Singer's head the footsteps of the sleepless creaked, the sneezes of those who had caught cold boomed, and he could hear, he thought, the meowing yawns of the weary.

Mendel Singer lighted the candle in the green bottle next to his bed, and went to the window. There he saw the red reflection of a night life which was going on somewhere afar, and the regularly recurrent, silver finger of a great searchlight which swept the sky as if desperately searching for God. Yes, and Mendel even saw a few stars, a few miserable stars, scattered from the main design of the heavens. Mendel remembered the clear, starry nights at home, the deep blue of the great spanning heavens, the softly curving sickle of the moon, the dark rustle of the forest firs, and the voices of the crickets and the frogs. It came to him that it would be easy now to leave the house, to wander out through the night, until he was again under the open sky and could hear the frogs and the crickets and the whimpering of Menuchim. Here, in America, he allied himself with the numerous voices in which the homeland sang and spoke to him – with the chirping of the crickets and the quacking of the frogs. But between them lay the ocean, thought Mendel. One must get into a ship, another ship again, and again travel twenty days and nights. Then he would be at home, with Menuchim.

His children begged him to leave this part of town, once and for all. But he was afraid. He did not want to be rash. Now, when everything was beginning to go well, one must not call down God's wrath. When had he seen better times? Why should he move to another neighbourhood? The few years which he expected to live he could pass in the company of the vermin.

He turned about. There lay Deborah, asleep. Formerly she had slept here, in this room, with Miriam. Now Miriam lived with her brother. Or, perhaps, with Mac, thought Mendel, swiftly, furtively. Deborah slept peacefully, half covered, a broad smile on her broad face. What is she to me? thought Mendel. Why do we live together? Our desire for each other is past, our children are grown and cared for, why am I with her? For the meals which she has cooked? It is written, it is not good for man to be alone. Thus we live together.

For a long time they had lived together; now it was just a question which would die first. Probably I, thought Mendel. She is healthy and her cares are few. She still hides money under some floor-board or other. She does not know that it is a sin to do so. Let her hide it!

The candle in the bottle neck burned to its end.

The night was over. One heard the first noises of the morning even before one saw the sun. Somewhere or other people opened creaking doors, blundering steps could be heard on the hallway stairs, the sky was a dull grey, and from the earth yellowish fumes arose, dust and sulphur from the gutters.

Deborah awoke, sighed, and said: 'It's going to rain! The gutter stinks; close the window.'

Thus began the summer days. In the afternoons,

Mendel did not come home to nap. He went to the children's playground. He found pleasure in the chirpings of a few sparrows, sat for a long time on a bench, drew with his umbrella crazy designs in the sand. The noise of the water, sprinkled from a long rubber hose over the little lawn, cooled Mendel Singer's countenance. He thought he could feel the water, and he dozed. He dreamed of the theatre, of acrobats in red and gold, of the White House, of the President of the United States, of Vanderbilt the millionaire, and of Menuchim.

One day Mac came. He said (Miriam accompanied him and translated) that at the end of July or in August he was going to Russia to fetch Menuchim.

Mendel guessed why Mac was going. Probably he wanted to marry Miriam. He was doing everything he could for the Singer family.

When I die, thought Mendel, Mac will marry Miriam. They are both waiting for my death. I have time. I am waiting for Menuchim.

It is June, a hot and especially long month. When will July finally come?

Towards the end of July Mac ordered his steamship ticket. They wrote to the Billes family. Mendel went into Skovronnek's shop, to tell his friends that his youngest son was also coming to America.

In the shop of the Skovronnek family many more people than usual had assembled. Each had a newspaper in his hand. The war had broken out in Europe.

Mac would not be able to go to Russia. Menuchim

would not be able to come to America. The war had started.

Had not Mendel Singer only now been freed from care? Care left him – and the war broke out.

Jonas was in the war, and Menuchim was in Russia.

Twice a week, in the evening, Sam and Miriam, Vega and Mac came to visit Mendel Singer. They took pains to hide from the old man the certain death of Jonas and the danger to Menuchim's life. It was as though they thought that they could divert Mendel's gaze, directed at Europe, towards their own good fortune and their own security. They put themselves between Mendel Singer and the war. And while he seemed to hear what they said, and to agree with their speculations – that Jonas probably had an office job, and that Menuchim would certainly be safe in a Petersburg hospital, because of his peculiar illness – he saw his son Jonas fall from his horse and hang caught in that barbed wire which the war correspondents described so vividly. And his little house in Zuchnow burned – and Menuchim lay in the corner and was burned with it.

Now and again he ventured a little remark: 'A year ago, when the letter came, I should have gone myself to Menuchim.'

No one knew how to answer this. Several times Mendel had made the remark, and always it was followed by the same silence. It was as though the old man, with this single sentence, extinguished the light in the room. It became dark, and no one could see where to point a finger. And after they had been quiet for a long time, they would arise and go.

But Mendel Singer, when he closed the door behind them and sent Deborah to bed, lighted a candle and began to sing one Psalm after another. He sang on good days and on bad ones. He sang when he had thanks to offer to Heaven, and when he feared it. Mendel's swaying movements were always the same. And only from his voice an observant listener might perhaps have recognized whether Mendel, the righteous, was thankful or burdened with anxiety.

In these nights fear shook him as the wind shakes a tender tree. And care lent him her own voice; in a stranger's voice, he sang the Psalms.

Finished, he closed the book, lifted it to his lips, kissed it and put out the light. But he found no peace. I have done too little, too little, he said to himself. Sometimes he was terrified at the thought that all he could do – the singing of the Psalms – was futile in face of the great storm in which Jonas and Menuchim were being wrecked. The cannons, he thought, are roaring; the flames are violent; my children are perishing. It is my fault, my fault! And I sing Psalms! It is not enough! It is not enough!

XII

ALL THE PEOPLE who had wagered in political discussions at Skovronnek's that America would stay neutral lost their bets.

It was early winter. At seven in the morning, Mendel Singer awakened. At eight he already stood in the street before his house. The snow was still hard and white, as at home in Zuchnow. But here it would melt quickly. In America it seldom lasted more than one night. The hurrying feet of the newsboys had already been kneading it. Mendel Singer waited until one of them passed. He bought a newspaper and went back into the house. The blue gas lamp was still burning. It lighted the morning, which was gloomy as night itself.

Mendel Singer unfolded the newspaper, which was greasy, sticky, and wet. He read the war news twice,

146

thrice, four times. He read that fifteen thousand Germans had been taken prisoner at one time, and that the Russians were resuming their offensive in Bukovina.

This alone did not satisfy him. He laid aside his glasses, polished them, and read the report from the front once again. His eyes seemed to sift the lines. Would not the names Sam Singer, Jonas, Menuchim, fall out of them?

'What's the news in the papers?' Deborah asked every morning.

'None at all,' answered Mendel. 'The Russians are winning, and the Germans are being taken prisoner.'

It was still. Over an alcohol lamp the tea was brewing. It sang almost as it did in the samovar at home. But the tea tasted different; it was rancid, an American tea, although the little package came wrapped in Chinese paper.

'One can't even drink the tea!' said Mendel, and wondered at himself for mentioning such trivialities. Perhaps he wanted to say something else. There was so much of importance in the world, and Mendel complained of the tea. The Russians were conquering, the Germans were being taken prisoner. But one heard nothing from Sam, and nothing from Menuchim.

Mendel had written two weeks before. And the Red Cross had reported that Jonas was missing.

'He is probably dead,' thought Deborah, in silence. Mendel thought the same. But they spoke for a long time over the exact meaning of the word 'missing', and always as though this word definitely shut out any possibility of death. They spoke as though it could mean only 'taken prisoner', or 'deserted', or 'wounded and in prison'.

Why did Sam wait so long to write? Well, he was probably on a prolonged march, or was being 'shifted'. At Skovronnek's they talked very wisely about 'shiftings' and 're-groupings'.

'One daren't say it aloud,' thought Mendel, 'but Sam oughtn't to have gone.'

Nevertheless, he uttered the second part of the sentence out loud. Deborah heard.

'You don't understand, Mendel,' said Deborah. All the arguments for Sam's participation in America's war, Deborah had gotten from Miriam. 'America isn't Russia, America is a real fatherland. Every decent person is duty-bound to go to war for his own fatherland. Anyhow, God be praised, he is with the regimental staff. They don't fall there. Because if they allowed all the high officers to die, they'd never win! And Sam, God be praised, is along with the high officers.'

'I gave one son to the Tsar. That ought to be enough.'

'The Tsar is different, and America is different!'

Mendel did not argue further. He had heard it all already. He still remembered the day when they departed, Mac and Sam. Both had sung an American song, marching in the middle of the street. In the evening, at Skovronnek's, the people had said: 'Sam, may his luck hold, is a fine-looking soldier.'

Perhaps America was a real fatherland, war a duty, cowardice shameful, and death – when one was attached to the regimental staff – out of the question. Just the same, thought Mendel, I am a father, I should have had a word to say. 'Sam, stay,' I should have said. 'I have waited many years for just a morsel of good fortune. Now Jonas is a soldier, who knows what will happen to Menuchim, you have a wife, a child, a business. Stay, Sam!' Perhaps he might have stayed.

Mendel stood at the window, as was his custom, with his back to the room. He looked straight ahead of him, at the Lemmels' broken window across the way, on the first floor. The window had been mended with brown cardboard. Underneath was a Jewish delicatessen store. There was a sign on the door in Hebrew – white, dirty letters on a pale blue background. Lemmel's son had also gone to the war. The whole Lemmel family went to night school and learned English. Evenings they went, like little children, carrying their copybooks. Perhaps they were right. Probably Mendel and Deborah should have gone to the school. America was a real fatherland.

It still snowed a little – slow, lazy, damp flakes. The Jews, with open umbrellas waving over their heads, began their promenade up and down. More and more came. They walked in the middle of the street; the last white scraps of snow melted under their feet; it looked as though they had to walk up and down by order of the authorities, until the snow had entirely disappeared. From his window Mendel could not see the sky. But he knew that it was gloomy. In all the windows opposite he saw the yellow reflection of gaslight. Gloomy were the heavens; in every house was gloom.

Soon a window opened here, and another there. One saw the busts of neighbour women. They hung red and white tickings, and naked yellow-skinned pillows out of the windows. Suddenly the whole street was colourful and gay. The neighbour women called loud greetings to one another. From inside the rooms sounded the rattle of plates and the cries of children. One might have believed it was peacetime if martial music had not been booming through the streets from Skovronnek's phonographs.

'When will it be Sunday?' thought Mendel. Once he had lived from one Saturday to the next; now he lived from one Sunday to the next. On Sunday visitors came – Miriam, Vega, the grandchild. They brought letters from Sam, or at least news of a general nature. They knew everything. They read the newspapers. They were running the business together, now. It was still going well; they were all industrious; they put money by, and waited for Sam's return.

Sometimes Miriam brought Mr. Glueck, the general manager, with her. She went dancing with Glueck; she went bathing with Glueck. Another Cossack! thought Mendel. But he said nothing.

'I can't go to the war, unfortunately,' sighed Mr. Glueck. 'I have a serious palpitation of the heart, the only thing which I inherited from my father of blessed memory.'

Mendel regarded Glueck's rosy cheeks, his little brown eyes, and his downy, coquettish moustache, which he wore in disregard of the mode, and with which he was constantly playing. He sat between Miriam and Vega. Once when Mendel suddenly stood up in the midst of a conversation, he thought that he saw one of Mr. Glueck's hands in Vega's lap, while the other rested on Miriam's thigh. Mendel went out into the street; he walked up and down until the guests departed.

'You act like a Russian Jew,' said Deborah, when he came back.

'I am a Russian Jew,' answered Mendel.

One day, a weekday early in February, while Mendel and Deborah were sitting at table, Miriam entered.

'Good day, Mother,' she said, and 'Good day, Father,' and stood there, still.

Deborah laid down her spoon and pushed back her plate. Mendel looked at both women. He knew that something extraordinary had happened. Miriam had come on a weekday, at a time when she should have been at business. His heart beat loudly. But he was self-possessed. It seemed to him that he could recall this scene. It had been played somewhere, once before. There stood Miriam, in her raincoat, and was dumb. There sat Deborah, the plate pushed far away from her, almost to the centre of the table, and outside it snowed, gently, flakily. The gas lamp burned with a feeble yellow light. It fought against the dark day, which was dank and weak, but nevertheless mighty enough to paint the whole room with its greyness. Mendel Singer remembered this light exactly. He had dreamed this scene. He knew, too, what was coming. Mendel knew everything, as though it had happened long ago, and as though the

151

pain of it had turned, many years ago, into grief. Mendel was quite calm.

Silence reigned for a few seconds. Miriam did not speak. It was as though she hoped that her father or mother would free her, by a question, from announcing her news. She stood still, and was silent. None of the three moved.

Mendel stood up and said: 'A misfortune has happened.'

Miriam said: 'Mac has come back. He has brought Sam's watch, and his last words.'

Deborah sat quiet, silent upon her chair, as though nothing had happened. Her eyes were dry and empty, like two little pieces of glass. She sat opposite the window, and it seemed as though she were counting the snowflakes.

It was so still, one heard the sharp ticking of the clock.

Suddenly Deborah began, very slowly, with stroking fingers, to rumple her hair. She pulled one strand after another over her face, which was pale and immobile as plaster. One after another she rent the strands of hair, one after another, in the same tempo in which, outside, the flakes were falling. Two, then three, white islands appeared amidst her hair, a few spots the size of a dollar where the naked scalp showed, and a few tiny drops of red blood. No one moved. The clock ticked, the snow fell, and Deborah quietly tore out her hair.

Miriam sank to her knees, buried her head in Deborah's lap, and moved no more. In Deborah's countenance not a feature changed. Her two hands tore –

now one, now the other – at her hair. Her hands were like pale, fleshy, five-footed animals, feeding themselves on hair.

Mendel stood, his arms folded over the back of the chair.

Deborah began to sing. She sang in a deep, male voice, which sounded as though there were an invisible singer in the room. The strange voice sang an old Jewish song without words, a dark lullaby, for dead children.

Miriam rose, pulled her hat straight, went to the door and let Mac in.

In uniform he looked larger than in his ordinary clothes. In his two hands, which he held before him like platters, he held Sam's watch, his pocketbook, his bill-fold.

These objects Mac laid slowly upon the table, directly in front of Deborah. He watched her for a while, tearing at her hair. Then he went to Mendel, laid both hands on the old man's shoulders, and wept, silently. His tears ran, a heavy rain, over his uniform.

It was still. Deborah's song had ceased. The clock ticked; evening sank suddenly over the world; the gas no longer shone with a yellow light, but was white. Outside the window-panes, the world was black; one could see no more snowflakes.

All of a sudden a suppressed scream came from Deborah's breast. It sounded like the rest of the melody which she had been singing, a broken, bursted note.

Then she fell from her chair. Deborah lay, a soft, crumpled mass, upon the floor.

Mac threw open the door, left it standing wide. It was cold in the room.

He came back, bringing a doctor, a little, bustling, grey-haired man.

Miriam stood across from her father.

Mac and the doctor carried Deborah to the bed. The doctor sat on the edge of the bed and said, 'She is dead.'

'Menuchim, too, is dead. Alone, among strangers,' thought Mendel Singer.

XIII

SEVEN DAYS ROUND Mendel Singer sat on a stool beside the clothes closet and looked at the window-pane where a scrap of white linen was hung as a symbol of mourning, and where day and night one of the blue lamps burned. Seven round days rolled one after the other, like great, slow black wheels, with no beginning and no end, round and endless as grief.

The neighbours came in turn: Menkes, Skovronnek, Rottenberg, and Groschel. They brought Mendel Singer hard-boiled eggs and the hard circular rolls called *beugels*, round things to eat, without beginning and without end, like the seven days of mourning.

Mendel spoke little with his visitors. He hardly noticed that they came and went. Day and night his door stood open, with the useless bolt thrust back. Who wished to come, came; who wished to go, went. This one or that tried to begin a conversation. But Mendel Singer avoided it. While the others spoke of living things, he talked with his dead wife.

'You are well off, Deborah,' he said to her. 'It is only sad that you have no son left to mourn you. I myself must say the prayer for the dead, but I will soon die, and no one will weep for us. Like two tiny specks of dust, we shall be scattered. Like two tiny tapers, we shall be extinguished. I have begotten children, your womb has borne them, death has taken them. Meaningless and full of poverty was your life.

'In my youth I took delight in your flesh; in later years I scorned it. Perhaps that was our sin. Because the warmth of love was not in us, but only the frost of familiarity, everything around us perished, or was ruined. You are well off, Deborah. God had pity on you. You are dead and buried. Towards me He shows no pity. For I am dead, and yet live. If you can, pray for me, that I shall be stricken from the book of the living.

'See, Deborah, the neighbours come to me, to comfort me. But although they are many, and they all think hard, they can find no comfort for my condition. My heart still beats, my eyes still see, my limbs still move, my feet still go. I eat and drink, pray and breathe. But my blood congeals, my hands are limp, my heart is empty. I am no longer Mendel Singer, I am but the remains of Mendel Singer. America has killed us.

'America is a real fatherland, indeed, but a death-dealing fatherland. What was life, with us, is death here.

The son, who at home was called Shemariah, here was called Sam. You are buried in America, Deborah, and I, too, will be buried in America.'

On the eighth day when Mendel Singer stood up from his mourning, his daughter-in-law came to him, with Mr. Glueck.

'Mr. Singer,' said Mr. Glueck, 'you must come with us immediately. The car is waiting below. Something has happened to Miriam.'

'Very well,' said Mendel Singer indifferently, as though one had announced to him that a room had to be papered. 'Very well, give me my coat.'

Mendel crept into his coat with his weak arms and went down the stairs. Mr. Glueck helped him into the car. They drove, and no word was spoken between them. Mendel did not ask what had happened to Miriam. Perhaps she too is dead, he thought calmly. Mac has killed her, out of jealousy.

For the first time he entered the dwelling of his dead son. Someone pushed him into a room. There lay Miriam, in a wide, white bed. Her hair was flowing loosely, in a sparkling blue-black wave over the white pillows. Her face glowed red, and her black eyes had wide, round red rims; circled with rings of flame were Miriam's eyes. A nurse sat near her. Mac stood in a corner, huge and motionless as a piece of furniture.

'There is Mendel Singer,' cried Miriam. She stretched her hand towards her father, and began to laugh. Her laugh lasted a few minutes. It sounded like the ringing of the clear, continuous signals at railway stations, and as though someone beat with a thousand brass hammers upon a thousand thin crystal glasses. Suddenly the laugh broke. For a second there was silence. Then Miriam began to sob. She pushed back the coverlet, her naked legs beat a tattoo, her feet beat in a quick, regular rhythm upon the soft bed, ever faster, ever more evenly, while her balled fists struck at the air in the same rhythm.

The nurse held Miriam fast, by main force. She became quieter.

'Good day, Mendel Singer,' said Miriam. 'You are my father. I can tell you all. I love Mac – there he stands – but I have deceived him. I slept with Mr. Glueck. Yes, with Mr. Glueck. Mac is my Mac; I like Mendel Singer, too, and if you like—'

Then the nurse clapped her hand over Miriam's mouth, and Miriam was silent.

Mendel Singer still stood in the doorway; Mac still stood in the corner. Both men gazed intently at each other. Since they could not communicate with each other in words, they spoke with their eyes.

'She has gone mad,' said Mendel Singer's eyes to the eyes of Mac. 'She could not live without men. She has gone mad.'

Vega entered and said, 'We have called a specialist. He ought to be here any moment. Since yesterday Miriam has been speaking strangely. She went walking with Mac, and when she came back she began to act in this queer way. The doctor must be here any moment.'

The doctor came. He was a German. He could talk with Mendel.

'We will have to take her to a sanatorium,' said the doctor. 'Your daughter, I am sorry to say, must go to a sanatorium. Wait just a moment. I will have to make it easier for her.'

Mac still stood in the room.

'Will you hold her fast?' asked the doctor. Mac held Miriam with his two great hands. The doctor drove a hypodermic needle into her thigh. 'She will soon be quiet,' he said.

The ambulance came, two bearers entered the room with a stretcher. Miriam slept. They bound her to the stretcher. Mac, Mendel, and Vega rode behind the ambulance.

'That has been spared you,' Mendel Singer addressed his wife Deborah, as they rode. 'I must go through with it, but I have known it all the time. Ever since the evening when I saw Miriam with the Cossack in the field I have known it. The Devil entered her. Pray for us, Deborah, that he will leave her again.'

Now Mendel sat in the waiting-room of the institution, surrounded by others waiting like himself. On a large table in the centre of the room was a vase full of yellow summer flowers and several illustrated magazines. But none of the waiting people smelled the flowers, and none turned the pages of the magazines. At first Mendel believed that all of the people who sat around him were insane, and he himself insane, like the rest. Then he saw, through the door of shining glass which separated this waiting-room from the whitewashed corridor, people in blue and white striped gowns being led by in pairs. First women, and then men, and sometimes one of the patients would show his wild, distorted, angry, wretched face in the waiting-room through a glass pane in the door.

All the waiting people would start; only Mendel remained still. Yes, it seemed strange to him that the people waiting did not wear striped garments, that he himself wore none.

He sat in a deep leather chair. His cap of black silk rep he had stuck upon one knee. His umbrella leaned, a loyal companion, against his chair. Mendel looked now at the people, now at the glass door, the periodicals, the insane patients, who still kept passing by outside – they were being taken to the baths – and at the golden flowers in the vase.

They were yellow cowslips; Mendel remembered that he often had seen them in the green meadows at home. The flowers came from home. He recollected them with pleasure. Those fields had been there, and these flowers. Peace had been at home there, youth had been at home there, and familiar poverty. In summer the sky had been pure blue, the sun pure heat, the grain pure yellow, the flies had gleamed greenly and had hummed warm little tunes, and high under the blue heavens the larks had trilled uninterruptedly.

Looking at the cowslips, Mendel Singer forgot that Deborah had died, Sam had fallen, Miriam had become mad, and Jonas was missing. It was as though he had only just lost his home, and with it Menuchim, the most loyal of all the dead, the farthest away of all the dead, the closest of all the dead. If only we had stayed there – thought Mendel – nothing would have happened. Jonas was right! Jonas, the most stupid of my children! He loved horses, and spirits, he loved the girls, and now he is missing. Jonas, I shall never see you again, I shall never be able to tell you that you were right to become a Cossack! 'Why do you always go wandering around in the world,' Sameshkin had said. 'The Devil drives you.' He was a peasant, Sameshkin, a shrewd peasant. Mendel had never wanted to go. Deborah, Miriam, Shemariah – they had wanted to go, to travel about in the world. One ought to stay at home, be fond of horses, drink spirits, sleep in the fields, let Miriam run with the Cossacks, and love Menuchim.

Have I become mad, Mendel's thoughts ran on, that I think this way? Does an old Jew think such thoughts? God has twisted my thoughts – the Devil thinks in me, as he speaks from my daughter, Miriam.

The doctor came in, drew Mendel into a corner, and said softly: 'Pull yourself together. Your daughter is very ill. There are lots of such cases now; the war, you understand, and the misery in the world – it's a bad time. Medicine doesn't know yet how to heal this illness. One of your sons is an epileptic, I have heard. You will pardon me – something of the sort seems to run in the family. We physicians call it "degenerative psychosis". It can pass. But it can also appear as an illness which we physicians call dementia: dementia praecox – but even the name is uncertain. Anyhow, it is one of the rare cases that we can do little for. You are a pious man, Mendel

Singer. The good God can help. Only pray zealously to the good God. By the way, would you like to see your daughter? Come with me!'

A bundle of keys rattled, a door slammed with a loud detonation, and Mendel walked through a long corridor past white doors with black numbers, like coffins set on end. Again the attendant's bundle of keys rattled, a coffin was opened, inside lay Miriam, asleep, with Mac and Vega standing beside her.

'We must go now,' said the doctor.

'Drive me right home, to my street,' commanded Mendel.

His voice sounded so hard, that all were shocked. They looked at him. His appearance did not seem to have changed. Nevertheless this was another Mendel. He was dressed exactly as he had been in Zuchnow, and during the whole time in America. In high boots, a half-length caftan, in his cap of black silk rep.

What had changed him so? Why did he appear to them all as taller and statelier? Why did his countenance exude so white and fearful a gleam? He almost seemed to tower above huge Mac. His Majesty, pain, thought the doctor, has entered the old Jew.

'Once,' began Mendel, in the car, 'Sam said to me that American medicine is the best in the world. Now it cannot help her. "God can help!" says the doctor. Tell me, Vega, have you ever seen God help a Mendel Singer? God can help!'

'You must live with us now,' sobbed Vega.

'I shall not live with you, my child,' answered Mendel.

'You will marry another husband, you should not be without a husband, your child should not be fatherless. I am an old Jew. Soon I shall die. Listen, Vega! Mac was Shemariah's friend; he loved Miriam. I know he is no Jew, but you should marry him. Not Mr. Glueck! Do you hear, Vega? Are you surprised that I speak so, Vega? Don't be. I am not insane. I am old. I have seen a few worlds perish, and at last I am wise. All the years long, I was a silly teacher. Now I know what I say.'

They came, helped Mendel out, led him to his room. Mac and Vega stood for a while, and did not know what to do.

Mendel sat down on a stool near the clothes closet and said to Vega, 'Don't forget what I told you. Now, go, my children.'

They left him. Mendel went to the window and watched them get into the car. It seemed to him that he must bless them, as though they were children who start out on a journey which may be very hard or may be very happy. I shall never see them again, he thought; then – I shall not give them my blessing, either. My blessing might be a curse, coming from me it could only harm them.

He felt light, lighter than ever in all his years. He had severed all relationships. It occurred to him that he had been alone for years. He had been alone since that moment when desire had ceased between his woman and himself. He was alone – alone. Wife and children had surrounded him and had hindered him from bearing his pain. Like useless poultices that do not aid healing, they had lain upon his wounds and had merely covered them. Now, at last, he indulged his misery in triumph! There was only one relationship still to be broken. He prepared to do it.

He went into the kitchen, ruffled newspapers together with kindling, and made a fire in the open stove. When the fire had reached a considerable height and breadth, Mendel walked with firm steps to the cupboard, and took from it the little red velvet sack which contained his phylacteries, his prayer shawl, and his prayerbooks.

He imagined to himself how these objects would burn. The flames would seize the yellowish shawl of pure sheep's wool, and destroy it with pointed, blue, greedy tongues. The glittering border of silver thread would slowly be reduced to embers, in tiny, glowing spirals. The fire would gently roll together the leaves of the books, change them into silvery ashes, and for a few seconds paint the black letters the colour of blood.

The leather corners of the binding would curl up; like the strange ears with which books listen they would stand up to hear what Mendel called after them as they died. He called a terrible song after them:

'It is over, all over; it is the end of Mendel Singer!' he cried, and his feet stamped in time to the tune, so that the floor-boards rumbled and the pots on the wall began to rattle.

'He has no son, he has no daughter, he has no wife, he has no country, he has no money! God said: I have punished Mendel Singer! For what has He punished him? Why has He not punished Lemmel, the butcher? Why not Skovronnek? Why not Menkes? He punishes only Mendel. Mendel has death, Mendel has madness, Mendel has hunger – all God's gifts are for Mendel! All, all over – it is the end of Mendel Singer!'

Thus stood Mendel before the fire, and bellowed, and stamped with his feet. He held the red velvet sack in his arms, but he did not cast it into the flames. A few times he lifted it high, but his arms let it sink again. His heart was angry against God, but in his sinews the fear of God still dwelt. Fifty years, day after day, these hands had spread the prayer shawl and folded it again, had unrolled the phylacteries, and bound them about his head and his left arm, had opened this book, paged in it, and closed it again. Now Mendel's hands refused to obey. Only his mouth did not refuse. Only his feet, which so often had danced to the glory of God, stamped in time to Mendel's paean of scorn.

Mendel's neighbours heard the crying and stamping and, when they caught sight of the blue-grey smoke through the cracks of his door, they knocked at Singer's door and cried that he should open for them. But he did not hear them. His eyes were filled with smoke from the fire, and in his ears sounded the noise of his great, painful exaltation. The neighbours were about to call the police, when one of them said: 'Let us call his friends. They are at Skovronnek's. Perhaps they can bring the poor fellow to his senses.'

When the friends came, Mendel actually did calm down. He pushed back the bolt and allowed them to come in, one after the other, as they were accustomed to enter Mendel's room: Menkes, Skovronnek, Rottenberg, and Groschel. They compelled Mendel to sit down on the bed, seated themselves beside him and before him, and Menkes said: 'What is the matter, Mendel? Why do you make such a fire? Why do you want to set the house on fire?'

'I want to burn more than a house and more than a person. You will be astonished when I tell you what I really intended to burn. You will wonder and say: Mendel is crazy, too, like his daughter. But I assure you, I am not crazy. For more than sixty years I have been mad, but today I am not.'

'Then tell us what you wanted to burn.'

'I want to burn God.'

At this, a cry burst simultaneously from all four listeners. They were not all pious and God-fearing, as Mendel had always been. All four had lived long enough in America; they worked on the Sabbath, their interest was in money, and the dust of the world already lay thick, high, and grey upon their ancient beliefs. Many ceremonials they had already forgotten; they had violated many laws, they had sinned with their heads and with their limbs. But God still dwelt in their hearts. And as Mendel blasphemed God, it seemed to them as though he had taken hold of their naked hearts with sharp fingers.

'Do not blaspheme, Mendel,' said Skovronnek, after a long silence. 'You know better than I, because you have studied more, that God's chastisements always have a hidden purpose. We do not know why we are punished.'

'But I know, Skovronnek,' answered Mendel. 'God is cruel, and the more one obeys Him the more brutally He treats one. He is mightier than the most mighty; with the nail of one of His little fingers He can wipe them out, but He does not do it. Only the weak He gladly destroys. The weakness of a man tempts His strength, and obedience awakens His scorn. He is a great, brutal *ispravnik*, a real Russian official. Follow the laws, and He says you have but done it for your own advantage. Break but one of His commandments, and He persecutes you with a hundred chastisements. Seek to bribe Him, and He brings a judgment against you. Deal uprightly with Him, and He is impatient for bribes. In all of Russia there is no worse *ispravnik*.'

'Think, Mendel,' began Rottenberg. 'Think of Job. The same sort of things happened to him as to you. He sat upon the naked earth, ashes upon his head, and his wounds hurt him so much that he writhed upon the ground like an animal. He, too, blasphemed God. And yet, it was only a test, after all. What do we know, Mendel, of what goes on up there? Perhaps the Evil One came to God, as he did then, and said: We must tempt one of the righteous. And God said: Just try it with my servant Mendel!'

'And there you see,' continued Groschel, 'that your complaints are unjust. For Job was not weak, when God tested him, but strong. And you, too, were not weak, Mendel. Your son had a big store, he was getting richer from year to year. Your son Menuchim was almost well, and he was just about to come to America. You were well and strong, your wife was well, your daughter was beautiful, and soon you would have found a husband for her!'

'Why do you break my heart, Groschel?' answered Mendel. 'Why do you tell me all that was, now, when I have nothing left? My wounds have not yet scarred, and you tear them open.'

'He is right,' said the other three, as though with one mouth.

And Rottenberg began: 'Your heart is torn, Mendel, I know. But because we dare to speak about everything with you, and since you know that we share your grief as though we were your brothers, will you be angry with us, if I ask you to think of Menuchim? Perhaps, dear Mendel, you tried to disturb God's plans, when you left Menuchim behind? A sick son was allotted to you, and you acted as though he were a wicked son.'

It was still. For a long time Mendel answered nothing at all. When he spoke again, it was as though he had not heard Rottenberg's words, for he turned to Groschel, and said:

'And why do you quote the example of Job? Have you really seen miracles with your own eyes? Miracles, such as were reported of Job, in the end? Shall my son Shemariah be resurrected out of the common grave in which he lies in France? Shall my son Jonas return alive from his long absence? Shall my daughter Miriam suddenly come home cured, from the insane asylum? And if she comes home, will she find a husband, and live

peacefully on, as though she had never been insane?
Shall my wife Deborah rise from her grave which is still
fresh? Shall my son Menuchim, in the midst of the war
in Russia, suddenly come here, even granted that he
still lives? For it is not true' – and here he turned again
to Rottenberg – 'that I left Menuchim behind out of
unkindness, to punish him. We had to leave for other
reasons, because of my daughter, who had begun to
run around with Cossacks – with Cossacks! And why was
Menuchim sick? His sickness itself showed that God was
wroth with me. It was the first blow, which I did not
deserve.'

'Although God can do all things,' began Menkes, the
most thoughtful of them all, 'it is probable that He no
longer performs the greatest miracles, because the
world is no longer worthy of them. And even if God
wanted to make an exception of you, the sins of the
others would count against you. For the others are not
worthy even to see a miracle happen to someone righteous. Thus Lot had to leave his home, and Sodom and
Gomorrah perished, and did not see the miracle of Lot.

'But today the world is everywhere populated – and
even if you leave your home the newspapers can report
what has happened to you. And so God can only perform moderate miracles today. But even those are great
enough, praise His name! Your wife Deborah cannot
live again, your son Shemariah cannot become alive.
But Menuchim is probably alive, and after the war you
will see him. Your son Jonas is probably in prison, and
after the war you will see him again. Your daughter

Miriam may be cured; the madness will be taken from her; she may be more beautiful than ever, and will get a husband, and bear you grandchildren. And you have one grandchild, Shemariah's son. Gather together all the love which you have had, up till now, for all the children and give it to this one grandchild! And you will be comforted.'

'Between me and my grandchild,' answered Mendel, 'the tie is broken. For Shemariah is dead, my son and the father of my grandchild. My daughter-in-law, Vega, will marry someone else; my grandchild will have another father, who is not my son. My son's house is not my house. I have nothing to do there. My presence brings misfortune, and my love draws a curse upon it, as a lonely tree in a level field draws down the lightning.

'But as far as Miriam is concerned, the doctor himself told me that medicine could not heal her sickness. Jonas is probably dead, and Menuchim was ill even when he was better off. In Russia, in the midst of so dangerous a war, he has certainly perished. No, my friends. I am alone, and I will remain alone. During all these years I have loved God, and he has hated me. All the arrows from His quiver have already hit me. He can but kill me. But He is too cruel for that. I shall live, live, live.'

'But His power,' interrupted Groschel, 'is in this world and in the next as well. Woe to you, Mendel, when you are dead!'

Then Mendel laughed outright, and said: 'I am not afraid of hell; my skin is already burned, my limbs lamed, and the evil spirits are my friends. I have already suffered all the tortures of hell. The Devil is kinder than God. Since he is not so mighty, he cannot be so cruel. I am not afraid, my friends!'

Then the friends were silent. But they did not wish to leave Mendel alone, and so they remained seated, dumb. Groschel, the youngest, went down to inform his own wife and the wives of the others that their husbands would not come home that night. He brought five more Jews to Mendel's dwelling, in order that they should be ten and could say the evening prayer. They began to pray. But Mendel Singer did not participate in the prayer. He sat motionless upon his bed. Even the prayer for the dead he did not say – and Menkes said it for him.

The five strangers left the house. But the four friends remained all night. One of the two blue lamps still burned. It was silent. This man or that slept where he sat, snored, and awoke, disturbed by his own noises, and nodded again.

Only Mendel did not sleep. With wide-open eyes he stared at the window, behind which the deep blackness of the night finally began to waver, was grey, then whitish. Six strokes sounded from inside the clock. Then the friends awoke, one after another.

And without consultation with each other, they grasped Mendel by the arms, and led him downstairs. They brought him into the back room of Skovronnek's shop, and laid him upon a sofa.

Here he slept.

XIV

FROM NOW ON Mendel Singer lived with the Skovronneks. His friends bought his wretched furniture. They left him only his bedding and the red velvet sack with the prayer utensils, which Mendel had almost burned. Mendel no longer touched the sack. Grey and dusty, it hung on a huge nail in Skovronnek's back room. Mendel Singer no longer prayed. Sometimes, to be sure, he participated when a tenth man was needed in order to complete the stipulated number of supplicants. Then he allowed them to count him as present. Sometimes, too, for a small consideration, he lent his phylacteries to this or that person.

People gossiped about him, saying that he went now and then into the Italian section, in order to eat pork and irritate God. In his fight against Heaven, the people with whom he lived took his part; although they were believers, they thought he was right. Jehovah had treated him too sorely.

War still raged in the world. Apart from Sam, Mendel's son, all members of this neighbourhood who had enlisted still lived. Young Lemmel had become an officer, and had had the luck to lose his left hand. He came home on leave and was the hero of his quarter. He gave to all Jews the feeling that they had a right to count America as their real home. He was staying in the service only to assist in the training of raw troops. Great as was the difference between young Lemmel and old Mendel Singer, the Jews of the neighbourhood linked them together in their minds. It was as though Mendel and Lemmel together had divided between them all the bad luck designed for all of them. And Mendel had lost more than just a left hand. If Lemmel was fighting the Germans, Mendel was fighting supernatural powers. Although they were convinced that the old man was no longer in full possession of his faculties, still the Jews could not help mixing a certain admiration with their sympathy, and feeling almost devout before such holy madness.

Undoubtedly Mendel Singer was a man marked by God. In the midst of those whose laborious days were undisturbed by terrors he lived as a pitiful witness of the cruel power of Jehovah. For many years he had lived his days like all the others, observed by few, by many not even noticed. Then one day he had been set apart, in a dreadful way. There were none, now, who did not know him. He spent the greater part of his days in the streets. It was as though it were part of his curse not only to suffer misfortune but to set an example, to wear the sign of his agony like a banner. And like a sentry over his own pain, he walked up and down in the middle of the street, greeted by all, presented with a small coin by some, questioned by many.

For the charitable gifts he returned no thanks, he hardly noticed the greetings, and questions he answered with yes or no. He rose early in the morning. In Skovronnek's back room no light entered; it had no window. He only felt the approach of morning, from a long way off. When the first noises began in the streets, Singer's day began. In an alcohol cooker the tea brewed. He ate with it some bread and a hard-boiled egg. He cast a shy but angry glance upon the sack with the holy objects, hanging on the wall. In the dark-blue shadows the sack looked like a still darker outgrowth of the shadow.

'I shall not pray,' thought Mendel. Yet he suffered because he did not pray. His rage hurt him, and the impotence of his rage. Although Mendel was angry with God, God still ruled the world. Hate could move Him no more than piety.

Filled with such and kindred thoughts, Mendel began his day. Once, he remembered, his awakening used to be light; the happy anticipation of his prayers had awakened him, and the desire to renew the familiar close contact with God. From the snug warmth of sleep he had entered with confidence and trust into the even more comfortable glow of prayer, as into a splendid, yet homelike room, in which a strong but smiling father lived. 'Good morning, Father,' Mendel had said – and believed that he heard an answer.

He had been deceived. The room was splendid but cold; the Father was strong but harsh. No sound issued from His lips but thunder.

Mendel Singer rolled up the iron shutters, and laid the sheet music, the song texts, the phonograph records, in the little show-window. Then he took a mouthful of water, sprinkled the floor, seized the broom, and swept together the debris of the preceding day. On a little shovel he carried the scraps of paper to the stove, made a fire, and burnt them. Then he went out, bought a few newspapers, and delivered them to some of the neighbours. He met the milkman and the early baker-boys, greeted them, and returned 'to business'.

Soon the Skovronneks arrived. They sent him on this errand or that. It was: 'Mendel, run out and buy a herring,' 'Mendel, the raisins for wine haven't been put up yet,' 'Mendel, you have forgotten the laundry,' 'Mendel, the ladder is broken!' 'A pane is out of the lantern!' 'Where is the corkscrew?' And Mendel ran out and bought a herring, put up raisin wine, fetched the wash and fixed the ladder and carried the lantern to the glazier and found the corkscrew. Sometimes the neighbours called him to look after the little children, when the moving picture show changed its programme or a new theatre opened.

And Mendel sat with the children of strangers, and, as

once with a light and tender finger he had set
Menuchim's basket swinging, so now, with a light and
tender tread of the foot, he rocked the cradles of children whose names he did not know. And as he rocked
he sang an old, old song:

'Say after me, Menuchim: In the beginning God created the heaven and the earth. Say after me,
Menuchim—'

It was in the month of Ellul, and the high holidays
were beginning. All the Jews of the neighbourhood
wanted to fix a temporary house of prayer in
Skovronnek's back room. (They did not like to go to
the synagogue.)

'Mendel, we will pray in your room,' said Skovronnek.
'What do you say?'

'You can pray,' said Mendel.

And he watched the Jews assemble and light the great
yellow wax candles, with their overhanging tufts of wick.
He himself helped every merchant to roll down his iron
shutters and lock his door. He saw how they all drew on
their white robes, so that they looked like corpses who
had risen from the dead to praise God. They drew off
their shoes and stood in their socks. They fell upon their
knees and rose again. The great golden-yellow candles
of wax, and the snow-white ones of paraffin, bent, and
dropped hot tears upon the prayer shawls, and
encrusted in no time. The white Jews themselves bent
like the candles, and their tears, too, fell upon the floor,
and dried.

But Mendel Singer stood, black and silent, in his

everyday clothes, in the background, near the door, unmoving. His lips were closed, and his heart was a stone. The song of Kol-Nidre rose like a hot wind. Mendel Singer's lips remained closed, and his heart a stone. Black and silent, in his everyday clothes, he kept to the background, close to the door. No one noticed him. The Jews went out of their way not to see him. A stranger was among them. This one or that thought of him, and prayed for him. But Mendel Singer stood erect in the doorway and hated God. They are all praying because they are afraid, he thought. But I do not fear Him. I am not afraid!

After they had all gone, Mendel Singer lay down on his hard sofa. It was still warm from the bodies of the supplicants. Forty candles still burned in the room. He did not dare to extinguish them, and he could not sleep while they burned. So he lay awake, all night long. He thought out exceptional, unheard-of blasphemies. He imagined himself going out, now, into the Italian section, buying pork in a restaurant, and bringing it back to eat, here, in the presence of the burning candles. He even undid his handkerchief and counted his coins, but he did not leave the room, he did not eat. He lay undressed on the sofa, with great sleepless eyes, and murmured:

'It is over, all over; it is the end of Mendel Singer! He has no son, he has no daughter, he has no wife, he has no money, he has no house, he has no God! All, all over; it is the end of Mendel Singer!'

The yellow and blue flames of the candles trembled

lightly. The hot waxen tears dropped with a hard sound upon the bases of the candlesticks, upon the yellow sand in the brazen mortars, on the dark-green glass of the bottles. The hot breath of the supplicants still lived in the room. The white prayer shawls still lay on the chairs that had been temporarily put in, awaiting the continuation of the service on the next day. The room smelled of wax and the glowing remnants of wicks.

Mendel left the room, opened the shop, walked into the open. It was a clear early autumn night. Nobody was in sight. Mendel walked up and down before the shop. The long, slow step of a policeman approached. Then Mendel went back into the shop. He still kept out of the way of men in uniform.

The holidays were over. Autumn came. Rain sang. Mendel bought herrings, swept the floor, fetched the wash, fixed the ladder, sought a corkscrew, put up raisin wine, and walked back and forth, in the middle of the street. For charitable gifts he returned no thanks, he hardly noticed greetings, and questions he answered with yes or no. In the afternoon, when people assembled to talk politics and read from the newspapers, Mendel lay on the sofa and slept. The talk of the others did not awaken him. The war did not concern him. The newest phonograph records sang to him in his sleep. He would awaken only when they had all gone, and it was still. Then he would talk for a while with old Skovronnek.

'Your daughter-in-law is going to marry again,' said Skovronnek once.

'Good,' answered Mendel.

'But she is going to marry Mac.'

'I advised her to.'

'Business is good.'

'It is not my business.'

'Mac has let us know he wants to help you, with money.'

'I don't want money.'

'Good night, Mendel.'

'Good night, Skovronnek.'

Exciting news was appearing in the newspapers which Mendel was accustomed to buy every morning. It flamed in their pages; against his will he was forced to notice its distant reflection – he wished to know nothing of it. In Russia there was no longer a Tsar. Good, let the Tsar go. In any case they could bring no news of Jonas and Menuchim, the newspapers. At Skovronnek's they were betting that the war would be over in a month. Good, let it be over. Shemariah would not come back. The administration of the asylum wrote that Miriam's condition had not improved. Vega sent the letter; Skovronnek read it aloud. 'Good,' said Mendel. 'Miriam will never get well.'

His old black caftan shimmered green on his shoulders, and, like a tiny drawing of the backbone, the seam was visible down the entire back. The skirts of his coat grew longer and longer. Now, when he walked, they did not touch the tops of his boots, but almost the ankles. His beard, which once had covered only his breast, reached to the lowest button of his caftan. The visor of his black, or rather greenish, rep cap had become soft and pliable, and hung limply over Mendel Singer's eyes, not unlike an old rag.

In his pockets Mendel Singer carried many things: little packets that people had given him, newspapers, implements with which he repaired broken odds and ends at Skovronnek's, spools of coloured string, brown paper, and bread. The weight of all these bowed Mendel's back even more, and, because the right pocket was usually heavier than the left, the old man's right shoulder was pulled awry. Thus he walked through the streets, oblique and bent, a wreck of a creature, with crooked knees and scuffling soles. The news of the world and the weekdays and feastdays of the others rolled past him, like carriages past an old house off the main road.

One day the war was really over. The neighbourhood was empty. Everyone had gone to see the peace celebration and the homecoming of the regiments. Many had commissioned Mendel to watch over their houses. He went from one flat to another, tested the bolts and locks, and returned home, to the store. From an unconscionable distance he thought he heard the festive sound of a happy world, the detonation of fireworks, the laughter of tens of thousands of men. A tiny, silent peace crept over him. His fingers combed his beard, his lips drew themselves into a smile, yes, there was even a little burst of laughter from his throat.

'Mendel will celebrate, too,' he whispered, and for the first time he approached one of the brown phonographs. He had seen how they wound the instrument. 'A record, a record!' he said. That very morning a returned soldier had been there and had brought half a dozen new records, new songs from Europe.

Mendel unpacked the top one, laid it carefully upon the instrument, meditated for a while trying to recall exactly how the thing was run, and finally set the needle to the disc. The apparatus croaked. Then the song began. It was evening; Mendel stood in the dark near the machine and listened.

Every day he had heard records, gay ones and sad ones, slow and fast, dark and light. But never had he heard a song like this one. It ran like a little brook and murmured softly; it was vast as the ocean and roared. Now I am hearing the whole world, thought Mendel. How is it possible that the whole world can be engraved on such a little disc? Then a silver flute tone melted into the violin music; it sewed itself around the velvety fabric of the violin playing like an accurate little hem. Mendel began, for the first time in long, to weep. Then the song was over. He played it again, and then a third time. Finally, he accompanied it in a hoarse voice, beating time, with a timid finger, upon the phonograph stand.

Skovronnek, returning, found him thus. He stopped the phonograph and said, 'Mendel, light the lamp! What are you playing here?'

'Look, Skovronnek, see what the song is called.'

'Those are the new records,' said Skovronnek. 'I bought them today. The song is called—' and Skovronnek put on his glasses, held the disc under the lamp, and read: 'The song is called *Menuchim's Song.*'

Mendel was suddenly faint. He had to sit down. He stared at the shining disc in Skovronnek's hands.

'I know what you are thinking,' said Skovronnek.

'Yes,' answered Mendel.

Skovronnek turned the crank again. 'A beautiful song,' said Skovronnek, his head on his left shoulder, listening.

Slowly the shop filled with late-returning neighbours. No one spoke. All listened to the song, and waved their heads in time. And they heard it sixteen times over, until they all knew it by heart.

Mendel was alone in the store. Carefully he locked the door on the inside, cleaned out the show-window, began to undress. At each step the song accompanied him. While he dropped off to sleep, it seemed to him that the blue and silver melody bound itself together with Menuchim's complaining whimper, with Menuchim's, his own Menuchim's only, long-unheard song.

XV

THE DAYS LENGTHENED. The mornings were so bright that
they even penetrated through the closed iron shutters
back into Mendel's windowless room. In April the street
awakened a good hour earlier. Mendel lighted the spirit
lamp, set on the tea, filled the little blue washbasin,
ducked his face in it, dried himself with the corner of
the towel which hung from the door latch, put up the
store shutters, took a mouthful of water and carefully
spat it over the floor, and regarded the tortuous pat-
terns which the bright stream from his pursed lips drew
in the dust. The clock had not yet struck six when the
water on the spirit lamp began to purr. Mendel stepped
outside. The windows in the street were opening as of
their own accord. It was spring.

It was spring. People were preparing for Easter, and in

all the houses Mendel helped. He ran the plane over the wooden table-tops to rid them of the profane remains of food accumulated during the year. He placed in the white partitions of the show-windows the cylindrical packages in which the layers of Passover bread were wrapped in bright red paper. He freed the Palestine wines of the cobwebs under which they had been resting in the cool cellars. He took apart the neighbours' beds, and carried them, piece by piece, into the courtyards, where the gentle April sun lured the vermin into the open and made possible their destruction with benzine, turpentine, and kerosene.

Out of pink and sky-blue tissue paper he cut with his shears fringes and round and angular designs, and fastened them with thumbtacks to the kitchen shelves, as an artistic setting for the china.

He filled tubs and barrels with hot water, and held great iron balls at the end of wooden rods in the fire of the stove, until they glowed red-hot. Then he immersed the balls in the barrels and tubs; the water hissed, and the vessels were clean, as was commanded by the precepts. In enormous mortars he pounded the Easter bread into flour, poured it into clean sacks, and bound them with blue ribbons.

All this he had once performed in his own house. Spring had come more slowly there than in America. Mendel remembered the ageing grey snow that edged the wooden pavement of the sidewalks at this time of year in Zuchnow. He remembered the crystal icicles which hung from the faucets; the sudden, soft rains which sang in the gutters of the eaves the whole night long. He remembered the distant thunder rolling far away behind the fir forest, the white rime which tenderly decked each bright blue morning. He remembered Menuchim, whom Miriam had stuck into a roomy vat in order to get him out of the way, and he remembered the hope that at last, at last, in this year the Messiah would come.

He had not come. He did not come, thought Mendel; he will not come. Let others await him. Mendel did not.

And yet to Mendel's friends and neighbours he seemed this spring, to be changed. They observed that he sometimes hummed a little song, and they caught a gentle smile under his white beard.

'He is becoming childish; he is already old,' said Groschel.

'He has forgotten everything,' said Rottenberg.

'He is happy that he will soon die,' said Menkes.

Skovronnek, who knew him best of all, was silent. But once, in the evening, before he went to sleep, he said to his wife:

'Since the new records arrived our Mendel is another man. I have caught him now and then winding up a phonograph himself. What do you think of that?'

'I think,' answered Mrs. Skovronnek impatiently, 'that Mendel is getting old and childish and soon will be no use to us.'

For some time she had been dissatisfied with Mendel. The older he became the less pity she felt for him. Gradually she was forgetting that Mendel had once been a well-to-do man, and her sympathy, which had been nourished by her respect (for she had little heart), died at the same time. She no longer called him, as at the beginning, Mister Singer, but simply Mendel, as indeed the whole world did. And whereas she had formerly given him orders with a certain reserve which showed that his obedience both honoured and shamed her, she now ordered him about so impatiently that her dissatisfaction with him was visible even before he acted. Although Mendel was not deaf, Mrs. Skovronnek raised her voice whenever she spoke with him, as though she feared that she would be misunderstood, and as though she sought to imply by her screaming that Mendel had carried out her orders badly when she had spoken to him in an ordinary tone of voice.

Her precautionary screams were the only thing that offended Mendel.

For he, so humiliated by Heaven, cared little for the careless and good-natured mockery of mankind, and was only insulted when people doubted his ability to understand.

'Hurry up, Mendel,' was the way Mrs. Skovronnek prefaced every order. He made her impatient; he seemed so slow.

'Don't yell so,' Mendel would occasionally answer. 'I hear you.'

'But you don't hurry; you take your time so.'

'I have less time than you, Mrs. Skovronnek, because I am older.'

Mrs. Skovronnek, who did not immediately grasp the

double meaning of his answer, nor the reprimand in it, but felt that she was being mocked, immediately turned to the nearest persons in the shop.

'Now, what do you say to that? He is getting old! Our Mendel is certainly getting old!'

She would have liked to accuse him of entirely other peculiarities, but she contented herself with calling attention to his age, which she held to be in itself a vice. When Skovronnek heard this sort of talk, he said to his wife:

'We will all be old some day. I'm just as old as Mendel, and you won't grow any younger yourself.'

'You can marry a young one if you like,' said Mrs. Skovronnek.

She was happy at last to have a ready-made reason for a marital quarrel. And Mendel, who knew very well the development of such disputes, and foresaw from the beginning that Mrs. Skovronnek's rage would finally vent itself against her husband and his friend, trembled for their friendship.

Today Mrs. Skovronnek was angry with Mendel for special reasons.

'Imagine,' she said to her husband. 'For several days now I have missed my meat chopper. I could swear that Mendel has taken it! But ask him, and he pretends to know nothing about it. He's getting older and older; he's like a child.'

As a matter of fact Mendel had taken Mrs. Skovronnek's meat chopper and hidden it. In secret he had long been working on a great plan, the last of his life.

187

One evening he thought he could carry it out. He pretended to nod, lying on the sofa, while the neighbours amused themselves at Skovronnek's. In reality Mendel did not doze at all. He lay in ambush and listened with closed eyelids until the last guest had departed. Then he drew the meat chopper from under the pillow of the sofa, hid it under his caftan, and glided swiftly into the darkening street. The street lamps were not yet lit; although from many windows yellow lamplight already shone.

Opposite the house in which he had lived with Deborah, Mendel Singer took his stand and spied at the windows of his former dwelling. A young married couple named Frisch lived there now; underneath they had opened a modern ice-cream parlour. Now the young people came out of the house. They locked the ice-cream parlour. They were going to a concert. They were saving, even stingy, industrious, and music-loving. The father of young Frisch had once been conductor in an orchestra in Kovno, which played at weddings. Today a philharmonic orchestra, just come from Europe, was playing. Frisch had spoken about it for days. Now they went out. They did not see Mendel.

He crept across the street and into the house, felt his way up along the familiar banister, and drew all the keys out of his pocket. He got them from the neighbours who made him watchman over their dwellings when they went to the moving pictures.

He opened the door without difficulty. He shoved the bolt to, laid himself flat on the floor, and began to knock on the floor-boards, one after another. It lasted a long time. He was tired, allowed himself a small pause, and then went on with his knocking. Finally, he heard a hollow sound, just at the place where Deborah's bed had once stood. Mendel cleaned the dirt out of the joint, loosened the board at all four edges with the meat chopper, and forced it up. He was not disappointed; he found what he was looking for. He grasped the strong, knotted handkerchief, hid it in his caftan, laid the floor-board back in place, and quietly let himself out. No one was on the stairs; no one had seen him.

Earlier than usual he closed the shop, rolling down the iron shutters. He lighted the great hanging lamp, and sat down in the circle of its light. He unknotted the handkerchief and counted its contents. Deborah had saved sixty-seven dollars, in bills and coins. It was much, but not enough for Mendel. If he added his own savings, the gifts and little fees for his work in the neighbours' houses, it made exactly ninety-six dollars. It was still not enough. 'A few months more!' whispered Mendel. 'I have time.'

Yes, he had time. He must live for quite a long time still. Before him lay the vast ocean. Once again he must cross it. The whole great sea waited for Mendel. All of Zuchnow and its surroundings waited for him: the barracks, the fir forest, the frogs in the swamp, and the crickets in the fields. If Menuchim were dead, he lay in the little cemetery and waited. And Mendel would lay himself down there, too. Before that he would enter Sameshkin's yard; he would no longer be afraid of the dogs – give him a wolf from Zuchnow, and he would not fear. Careless of beetles and snakes, of toads and grasshoppers, he would be prepared to lie upon the naked earth. The church bells would sound for him, and remind him of the listening light in Menuchim's foolish eyes.

Mendel would say: 'I have come home, dear Sameshkin. Let others wander through the world. My worlds are dead, I have come back in order to sleep for ever here.'

The blue night is stretched over the land, the stars glitter, the frogs croak, the crickets chirp, and over there, in the dark forest, someone sings Menuchim's song.

So Mendel went to sleep, the knotted handkerchief in one hand.

The next morning he went into the Skovronneks' flat, laid the meat chopper on the cold kitchen stove, and said: 'Here, Mrs. Skovronnek, is the chopper; it is found.'

He tried to hurry away, but Mrs. Skovronnek began: 'Found, is it? That wasn't hard! You hid it yourself! Besides, you certainly slept soundly last evening. We stopped again at the shop and knocked. Did you hear? Frisch, from the ice-cream parlour, has something very important to say to you. You should go over to him right off.'

Mendel was scared. So, someone had seen him yesterday; perhaps someone else had robbed the flat, and they suspected Mendel! Perhaps, too, it wasn't Deborah's savings, but Mrs. Frisch's that he had taken, and he had robbed her! His knees trembled.

'Let me sit down,' he said to Mrs. Skovronnek.

'You can sit just two minutes,' she said. 'Then I must start cooking.'

'What sort of important thing is it?' he inquired. But he knew that the woman would tell him nothing. She gloated over his curiosity, and was silent. Then, when Mendel's two minutes were up, she said:

'I don't concern myself with other people's business. Just go to Frisch.'

Mendel went out, resolved not to go to Frisch's. It could only be something bad. Frisch would come soon enough himself. He waited.

But in the afternoon Skovronnek's grandson came visiting. Mrs. Skovronnek sent Mendel for three portions of strawberry ice cream. Mendel entered the shop faint-heartedly. Luckily Mr. Frisch was not there. His wife said:

'My husband has something very important to tell you. You must surely come this afternoon.'

Mendel acted as though he had not heard. His heart was beating stormily, as though it would spring from his breast. He held it with both hands. In any case something evil was threatening him. He would tell the truth; Frisch would believe him. If he didn't believe him he would go to jail. Well, and what of it? In prison, he would die. Not in Zuchnow.

He could not leave the vicinity of the ice-cream parlour. He walked up and down before the shop. He saw Frisch return home. He wanted to wait longer, but his feet hurried, by themselves, into the shop. He opened the door, setting a shrill bell ringing, and found no strength to close it, so that the alarm went on and Mendel stood deafened by its violent noise, incapable of moving.

Mr. Frisch himself closed the door. And in the quiet which followed, Mendel heard Mr. Frisch say to his wife:

'Quick, a raspberry soda for Mr. Singer.'

How long had it been since anyone had said 'Mister Singer' to Mendel? In this moment he realized for the first time that people had been calling him Mendel in order to humiliate him. It's a mean joke of Frisch's, he thought. The whole neighbourhood knows that this young man is stingy; he knows that I won't pay for the raspberry soda. I won't drink it.

'Thanks, thanks,' said Mendel. 'I don't care for anything.'

'You mustn't turn us down,' said the woman, smiling.

'He won't refuse me,' said young Frisch.

He drew Mendel to one of the thin-legged iron tables and pressed him into a wicker chair. He himself sat down on an ordinary wooden chair, pulled himself close to Mendel, and began:

'Yesterday, Mr. Singer, I was at the concert, as you know.'

Mendel's heart palpitations started again. He leaned back and took a swallow, in order to sustain life.

'Now,' Frisch went on, 'I have heard a lot of music, but this was like nothing in the world. Thirty-two musicians, understand, and almost all of them from around our part of the world. And they played Jewish melodies, understand? It warmed the heart; I cried. Almost the whole audience cried. And at the close they played *Menuchim's Song*, Mr. Singer. You know it from the phonograph record. A beautiful song, isn't it?'

'What does he want,' thought Mendel. 'Yes, yes, a lovely song.'

'During the intermission, I went back to the musicians' room. It was crowded. Everybody wanted to meet the musicians. This one and that discovered a friend, and I, too, Mr. Singer – I, too!'

Frisch paused. People entered the shop. The bell rang shrilly.

'I found – but have a drink, Mr. Singer! – I found my own cousin, Berkovitch, from Kovno. The son of my uncle. And we kissed. And we talked. And suddenly Berkovitch said, "Do you know an old man – named Mendel Singer?"'

Frisch waited again. And Mendel Singer did not move. He accepted the fact that a certain Berkovitch had asked after an old man, Mendel Singer.

'Yes,' said Frisch, 'I answered that I knew a Mendel Singer from Zuchnow. "That's he," said Berkovitch. "Our conductor is a great composer, still young, and a genius; he wrote most of the pieces that we play. His name is Alexis Kossak, and he is also from Zuchnow."'

'Kossak?' answered Mendel. 'My wife was born a Kossak. He must be a relative.'

'Yes,' said Frisch, 'and it seems that this Kossak is looking for you. Probably he has news for you. And I should ask you if you would like to hear it. You can either go to his hotel, or I will write Berkovitch your address.'

Mendel felt at the same moment relieved and depressed. He drank the raspberry soda, leaned back, and said:

'Thank you, Mr. Frisch. But it is not so important. This man Kossak will tell me all sorts of sad things that I already know. And apart from that, I will tell you the truth: I had wanted for some time to get your advice. Your brother has a steamship agency, hasn't he? I want to go home, to Zuchnow. It is no longer Russia; the world has changed. What does a ticket cost today? And what documents would I have to have? Talk with your brother, but don't tell anyone else.'

'I will inquire,' answered Frisch. 'But you certainly haven't enough money. And at your age! Perhaps this Kossak will tell you something. Perhaps he will take you with him! He is only staying for a short time in New York. Shan't I give Berkovitch your address? Because, if I know you, you won't go to the hotel.'

'No,' said Mendel. 'I won't go. Write him if you like.'

He got up to depart. Frisch pressed him into his chair again.

'Just a moment, Mr. Singer,' he said. 'I brought the programme with me. This Kossak's picture is on it.'

From his waistcoat pocket he drew a large programme, unfolded it, and held it for Mendel to see.

'A good-looking young man,' said Mendel. He looked at the photograph. Although the picture was worn, the paper dirty, and the portrait seemed about to dissolve into a hundred thousand tiny molecules, it looked up from the programme with vitality. He wanted to return it immediately, but he held it and stared. Under the black hair the forehead was broad and white as a smooth, sunny stone. The eyes were large and clear. They looked directly at Mendel Singer. He could not free himself from them. They made him happy and light-hearted, Mendel believed. He saw the light of their intelligence. They were old, and at the same time young. They knew everything; the whole world reflected itself in them. It seemed to Mendel Singer, looking at these eyes, that he himself was younger; he was a youth who knew nothing. He must learn everything from these eyes.

Years ago, when he had begun the study of the Bible, these had been the eyes of the prophets. Men to whom God Himself had spoken had such eyes. They knew all, they betrayed nothing; they were full of light.

Mendel looked at the picture for a long time. Then he said, 'I will take it home with me, if you permit, Mr. Frisch.' And he folded up the paper and went.

He went around the corner, unfolded the programme, looked at it again, and stuck it in his pocket. A long time seemed to have elapsed since he entered the ice-cream parlour. The few thousand years which shone in Kossak's eyes lay between, and the years when Mendel was still so young that he could imagine the countenances of the prophets. He wanted to turn around, to ask where the concert hall was, where the orchestra was playing, and to go in. But he was ashamed. He went to Skovronnek's shop and told them that a relative of his wife was in America and looking for him. He had given Frisch permission to tell his address.

'Tomorrow evening you will eat with us, as you do every year,' said Skovronnek. It was the first Passover evening. Mendel nodded. He would rather remain in his back room; he knew the oblique glance of Mrs. Skovronnek, and the calculating hands with which she apportioned to Mendel his soup and fish. It is the last time, he thought. In another year I shall be in Zuchnow, living or dead; rather dead.

He was the first guest to arrive the next night, but the last to sit down to table. He came early, in order not to offend Mrs. Skovronnek; he took his place last in order to show that he considered himself the least of those present. Already they sat about the table – the hostess, both of Skovronnek's daughters with their husbands and children, a strange music salesman, and Mendel. He sat at the end of the table, upon which a planed board had been laid to make it longer. Mendel's concern was not only to maintain the peace, but to keep the precarious extension balanced on the table-top.

When a plate or tureen had to be set on the end of the board, Mendel held it fast. Six thick snow-white candles burned in the silver candlesticks upon the snow-white tablecloth, from the starched surface of which were reflected the six lights. Like white and silver watchmen, all of the same height, the candles stood before Skovronnek, the host, who sat in a white robe upon a white cushion, leaning against another cushion, a purified king upon a purified throne. How long had it been since Mendel in the same costume had ruled the feast in the same fashion? Today he sat, bent and broken, in his greenish coat, at the far end of the table, the least among the guests, concerned with appearing to be modest, a miserable support for the festivities.

The unleavened bread lay covered with a white napkin, a snowy mound beside the juicy green of the kale, the dark red of beets, and the acid yellow of the horseradish root. The books with the account of the exodus of the Jews from Egypt lay open before each guest. Skovronnek began to chant the legend, and all repeated his words, caught up with him, and sang in unity the comforting, smiling melody, a chorused account of the various miracles, numbered over and over again, and always manifesting the same virtues of God: His greatness, His goodness, His compassion, His mercy towards Israel, His anger with Pharaoh.

Even the music salesman, who could not read the Holy Writ and did not understand the customs, could not resist the melody, which wooed him with every verse, caressed him, drew him into its net, so that he began to hum it unwittingly. And even Mendel became milder towards Heaven, which four thousand years ago had generously lavished such marvellous miracles, and it was as though, because of God's love for his whole people, Mendel could almost be reconciled to his own fate. He still did not participate in the song, but his body swung backwards and forwards, cradled in the song of the others. He heard Skovronnek's grandchildren singing in their clear voices, and recalled the voices of his own children. He still saw the helpless Menuchim raised on his unaccustomed chair at the festive table. Only the father had, from time to time during the singing, cast a hasty glance upon his youngest and least gifted son, had seen the listening light in his foolish eyes, and had felt how the little one tried in vain to express what sounded in him, and to sing what he heard.

It was the only evening in the year when Menuchim wore a new suit, like his brothers, the white collar of his shirt with its bright red edging about his flabby double chin. When Mendel reached him the wine, he drank half the glass, with one greedy draught, then sneezed, and distorted his face in an ineffectual attempt to laugh or to cry; who knew which?

Mendel thought of these things as he swayed to the song of the others. He saw that they were already far ahead of him. He turned over a few pages, and prepared to stand up and to free the corner of the plates so that there would be no catastrophe when he let go of it. For the moment was approaching when the red beaker of wine would be filled, and the door opened in order to admit the prophet Elijah. The dark-red glass was waiting, the six candles glittered in its curved surface. Mrs. Skovronnek lifted her head and looked at Mendel. He stood up, glided to the door, and opened it. Now Skovronnek sang the invitation to the prophet. Mendel waited until he was finished, for he did not want to go to the door twice. Then he closed the door, braced a supporting fist under the table-leaf, and the singing went on.

Hardly a minute had passed after Mendel had seated himself, when a knock sounded. Everyone heard the knock, but everyone thought he was mistaken. On this evening all their friends were at home, the streets of the quarter were empty. At this hour no visitor was possible. It was certainly the wind which knocked.

'Mendel,' said Mrs. Skovronnek, 'you haven't closed the door properly.'

Then the knock sounded again, longer and more clearly. All waited. The smell of the candles, the flush of the wine, the unusual yellow light, and the old melody had brought grown-ups and children to the point where they almost awaited a miracle, so that they held their breaths for a moment, and stared at each other, perplexed and pale, as though they asked themselves whether the prophet were indeed at the door. And so there was silence, and no one trusted himself to move. Finally Mendel stirred. Again he pushed the plates towards the centre of the table. Again he glided to the door and opened it . . . There in the half-dark passage stood a tall stranger who wished him good-evening, and asked whether he might enter. Skovronnek got up from his cushions with some difficulty. He went to the door, looked at the stranger, and said: 'If you please,' as he had learned one should do, in America.

The stranger entered. He wore a dark overcoat. His collar was turned up, he kept his hat on his head, obviously out of reverence for the ceremony into the midst of which he had stepped, and because all the men present sat with their heads covered.

'He is a sensitive person,' thought Skovronnek. And without saying a word, he unbuttoned the stranger's coat. The man bowed and said:

'My name is Alexis Kossak. I beg your pardon. I sincerely beg your pardon. I had been told that I would find here a certain Mendel Singer from Zuchnow. I should like to speak with him.'

'I am he,' said Mendel, approached the guest, and lifted his head. His forehead but reached to the shoulder of the stranger. 'Mr. Kossak,' he continued, 'I have heard of you already. We are relatives.'

'Lay off your things, and sit down with us at the table,' said Skovronnek.

Mrs. Skovronnek rose. They all pushed together. They made a place for the stranger. Skovronnek's son-in-law set another chair at the table. The stranger hung his coat on a nail, and sat down opposite Mendel. They placed a glass of wine before the guest.

'Do not let me interrupt you,' bade the stranger. 'Please go on with your prayers.'

They continued. Silent and slender, the guest sat in his place. Mendel gazed at him without stopping. Alexis Kossak's gaze at Mendel Singer was unbroken. Thus they sat opposite each other, fanned by the singing of the others, but separated from them.

They both felt grateful that the presence of the others kept them from talking to each other. Mendel sought the stranger's eyes. If Kossak cast them down, it seemed to the old man that he must beg him to open them again. In this countenance, everything was strange to Mendel Singer except the eyes behind the rimless glasses, which were familiar. His gaze always strayed back to them, like a homecoming to well-known lights behind

200

windows, in the unfamiliar landscape of the narrow, pale, and youthful face.

His lips were thin, tight, and smooth.

'Were I his father,' thought Mendel, 'I should say, "Smile, Alexis!" '

He drew the programme quietly from his pocket, unfolded it under the table in order not to disturb the others, and handed it to the stranger. He took it and smiled, thinly, tenderly, and for but a moment.

The singing ended, and the feast began. Mrs. Skovronnek pushed a plate of soup before the guest, and Mr. Skovronnek bade him eat with them. The music salesman began a conversation in English with Kossak, of which Mendel understood nothing. Then the salesman declared to them all that Kossak was a young genius, that he was staying only a week in New York, and that he would be happy to present all of them with free tickets to his concert.

Other conversations failed to start. They ate in unfestive haste, approaching the close of the celebration, and every second bite was accompanied by a polite word from the host or from the guest. Mendel did not speak. To please Mrs. Skovronnek he ate even faster than the others, not to contribute to any delay.

All of them greeted the end of the feast, and eagerly began the recitation of the miracles. Skovronnek struck an even quicker rhythm; the women could hardly follow him. But when he came to the Psalms, his voice changed, as did the tempo and the melody, and the words which he sang sounded so enchanting that even

201

Mendel, at the end of each strophe, joined in the Hallelujah! Hallelujah! He shook his head so that his long beard swept over the open leaves of the book, and a gentle rustling was audible, as though the beard of Mendel participated in the prayer which the mouth of Mendel so reluctantly celebrated.

Soon they were finished. The candles had burned to half their size, the table was no longer smooth and festive, spots and crumbs of food were visible on the white cloth and Skovronnek's grandsons were already yawning. At the close the book was lifted. In a loud voice Skovronnek repeated the traditional wish: 'Next year in Jerusalem!' They all repeated it, closed the books, and turned to the guest.

Now it was Mendel's turn to question the guest. The old man cleared his throat, smiled, and said, 'Now, Mr. Alexis, what have you to tell me?'

In a low voice the stranger began. 'You should have heard from me long ago, Mr. Mendel Singer, had I had your address. But after the war no one knew it. Billes's son-in-law, the musician, died of typhus; your house in Zuchnow stood empty, for Billes's daughter went to her parents who already lived in Dubno; and in Zuchnow, in your house, Austrian soldiers were quartered. Now, after the war, I wrote to my manager here, but the man was not clever enough to find you.'

'Too bad about Billes's son-in-law,' said Mendel, and thought of Menuchim.

'And now,' continued Kossak, 'I have some pleasant news.'

202

Mendel lifted his head. 'I bought your house from old Billes before witnesses, and on the basis of an official estimate of its worth. And I will pay you the money.'

'How much is it?' asked Mendel.

'Three hundred dollars!' said Kossak.

Mendel gripped his beard and combed it tremblingly with spread fingers.

'Thank you,' he said.

'As far as your son Jonas is concerned,' said Kossak, 'he disappeared in the year 1915. No one had news of him, either in Petersburg, Berlin, Vienna, or in the Swiss Red Cross. I asked or had inquiries made everywhere. But two months ago I met a young man in Moscow. He had just escaped over the Polish border, for, as you know, Zuchnow now belongs to Poland. And this young man had been in Jonas's regiment. He told me that he had once heard, by accident, that Jonas was alive and fighting in a White Guard regiment. In that case it would of course have been difficult to get any news from him. But you need not yet give up hope.'

Mendel wanted to open his lips to ask after Menuchim. But his friend, Skovronnek, who anticipated Mendel's question and was certain of a sad reply, was anxious to avoid unhappy talk on this particular evening, or to postpone it, at least, as long as possible, so he interrupted the old man, and said:

'Now, Mr. Kossak, that we have the pleasure of having so distinguished a guest as you, won't you tell us something, perhaps, of your own life? How does it happen that you escaped the war, the revolution, and all dangers?'

The stranger had obviously not expected this question, for he did not answer immediately. He cast down his eyes, as one who was ashamed or had to think, and answered only after a long pause.

'I have not gone through anything special. As a child I was sick for a long time. My father was a poor teacher, like Mendel Singer, to whose wife I am related. It is not the time, just now, to explain the relationship more exactly. To be brief, because of my illness, and because we were poor, I was sent to a great city, to a public medical institute. And there I was well treated, a physician took a special interest in me, I was cured, and the doctor took me into his own house.

'There' – and here Kossak's head sank, and it was as though he spoke to the table, and everyone held his breath in order to hear his exact words – 'there I sat down at the piano one day and played out of my head my own songs. And the doctor's wife wrote notes to these songs. The war was my good fortune. For through it I came to perform military music, and became the leader of a band, stayed the whole time in Petersburg, and even played a few times before the Tsar. After the revolution my band went abroad with me. A few left us, new ones came; in London we made a contract with a concert agency, and thus my orchestra came into being.'

They all continued to listen, although the guest spoke no more. But his words still lingered in the room, and now struck first this one and then that. Kossak spoke the Yiddish jargon badly, he interspersed half Russian sentences in his account, and Mendel and the

Skovronneks missed many details but grasped the sense of it all. Skovronnek's sons-in-law, who had come as small children to America, understood less than half of what was said, and had their wives translate the stranger's words into English. The music salesman then went over Kossak's biography again, in order to impress it upon them.

The candles had burned down in the candlesticks to short stumps; it was dark in the room; the grandchildren slept in their chairs with their heads on the side, but no one made a move to go. Yes, Mrs. Skovronnek even fetched two candles, stuck them upon the old stumps, and thus reopened the evening. Her ancient respect for Mendel Singer reawakened. This guest, who was a great man, had played before the Tsar, wore a remarkable ring on his little finger and a pearl in his cravat, and was dressed in a suit of good European stuff – she knew what was what, because her father had been a draper – this guest could hardly go with Mendel into the back room. Yes, to the astonishment of her husband, she said:

'Mr. Singer! It is a good thing that you came to us this evening. Usually' – and she turned to Kossak – 'he is so modest and sensitive that he refuses my invitations. And yet he is like the oldest child in our house.'

Skovronnek broke in. 'Make us some more tea!' And as she stood up, he said to Kossak: 'We all have known your songs for some time. *Menuchim's Song* is yours, isn't it?'

'Yes,' said Kossak. 'It is by me.'

It seemed as though this question was unwelcome to him. He looked quickly at Mendel and said: 'Your wife is dead?'

Mendel nodded.

'And as far as I know, you have a daughter?'

In Mendel's place Skovronnek answered: 'Unfortunately, her mother's death, and that of her brother Sam made her insane, and she is in the asylum.'

The stranger bowed his head. Mendel rose and went out.

He wanted to ask after Menuchim, but he had not the courage. He knew the answer in advance. He put himself in the place of the guest and answered himself: 'Menuchim is long since dead. He perished miserably.' He practised this sentence, tasted in advance its whole bitterness, in order, when he really heard it, to be able to sit quietly. And because he still had a shy hope in his heart, he sought to kill it. If Menuchim were alive – he said to himself – the stranger would have told me right away. No! Menuchim is long since dead. And now I will ask him, so that this stupid hope will come to an end at last!

But still he did not ask. He sat silent for a while, and the noisy activity of Mrs. Skovronnek, who was busy in the kitchen with the tea kettle, gave him an excuse to leave the room, in order to help the hostess.

But she sent him back. He had three hundred dollars and a distinguished relative.

'It isn't right for you, Mister Mendel,' she said. 'Don't leave your guest alone.'

Anyhow, she was already finished. With full tea glasses on a broad tray, she entered the room followed by Mendel. The tea was steaming. Mendel had finally made up his mind to inquire after Menuchim. Skovronnek, also, felt that the question could no longer be postponed. He would rather ask himself; Mendel, his friend, should not add to the pain which the answer would cause, the misery of asking it.

'My friend, Mendel, had another poor, sick son, named Menuchim. What has happened to him?'

Again the stranger did not answer. He poked around in the bottom of his glass with his spoon, crushed the sugar, and gazed at the pale brown glass as though he would read the answer in it. And with the spoon still held between his thumb and forefinger, his narrow brown hand gently waving to and fro, he said finally, in an unexpectedly loud voice, as though by sudden decision:

'Menuchim is alive!'

It did not sound like an answer; it sounded like a cry. At once a laugh burst from Mendel Singer's breast. Everyone started, and stared at the old man. Mendel sat, leaning back in his chair, and shook, and laughed.

He is so bent that he no longer can touch the whole of the chair back. Between the back of the chair and Mendel's old neck (white hairs curl over the shabby collar of his coat) there is a wide space. Mendel's long beard moves violently; it almost flutters, like a white flag. And it, too, seems to laugh. From Mendel's breast comes now a rumbling, now a tittering. Everyone is scared.

Skovronnek rises with some difficulty from his swollen cushions, hampered by his long white robe, and, going to Mendel, bends over him, taking both his hands in his. Now Mendel's laughter turns to weeping. He sobs, and the tears flow over his old, half-veiled eyes, into the wild beard, losing themselves in the tangled brush; others remain for a while, hanging in the hair of his beard, round and full as drops of glass.

Finally Mendel becomes quiet. He looks straight at Kossak, and repeats:

'Menuchim is alive?'

The stranger looks at Mendel calmly and says:

'Menuchim lives. He is alive, he is well, he is even prosperous.'

Mendel folded his hands, lifting them as high as he could towards the ceiling. He tried to stand up. He had the feeling that now he must stand up, stand straight, grow, become taller and taller, higher than the house, and with his hands touch the skies. He can no longer unclasp his folded hands. He looks at Skovronnek, and the old friend knows what he has to ask, in Mendel's stead.

'Where is Menuchim now?' asks Skovronnek.

And slowly Alexis Kossak answers:

'I am Menuchim.'

All arise suddenly from their places. The children, who were already asleep, awake and burst into tears. Mendel stands up so violently that behind him the chair falls down with a loud crash. He walks, he runs, he hastens, he skips to Kossak, who alone has remained seated. There is a great commotion in the room. The candles begin to flicker as though they are moved by a sudden wind. On the wall flutter the shadows of the standing people. Mendel sinks down before Menuchim; he searches with impatient mouth and waving beard for the hands of his son; his lips kiss whatever they touch, the knees, the legs, the waistcoat of Menuchim.

Mendel stood up at last. He lifted his hands, and as though he were blind, began to touch his son's face, with eager fingers. The blunt old fingers glided over Menuchim's hair, over his smooth, broad brow, over the cold glass in his spectacles, over the thin closed lips. Menuchim sat quietly, and did not move. All present surrounded Menuchim and Mendel. The children cried, the candles flickered, the shadows on the wall merged into a dark cloud. No one spoke.

Finally, Menuchim's voice sounded.

'Stand up, Father,' he said, and grasped Mendel under the arms, lifted him high, and seated him upon his knees, like a child. The others drew away. Now Mendel sat upon the lap of his son, and smiled into the face of each person in the circle. He whispered:

'Pain will make him wise, ugliness good, bitterness mild, and sickness strong!'

Deborah had said it. He heard her voice still.

Skovronnek left the table, laid his robe aside, drew on his coat and said: 'I shall be back immediately.'

Where was Skovronnek going? It was not yet late; the friends were still at their tables. He went from house to house, to Groschel, Menkes, Rottenberg. He would find them all, still at their tables.

'A miracle has happened! Come with me and witness it!'

He led all three to Mendel. On the way they met Lemmel's daughter, who had been accompanying her guests. They told her about Mendel and Menuchim. Young Frisch, who had gone out for a little walk with his wife, also heard the news. And thus a few learned what had happened. Below, before Skovronnek's house, stood, as proof, the automobile in which Menuchim had come. A few people opened their windows and looked at it. Menkes, Groschel, Skovronnek, and Rottenberg, entered the house. Mendel went towards them and silently pressed their hands.

Menkes, the most thoughtful of them all, was spokesman.

'Mendel,' he said, 'we have come to visit you in your good luck as we visited you in your misfortune. Do you remember how crushed you were? We tried to comfort you, but we knew it was in vain. Now you in the flesh experience a miracle! As we mourned with you then, so we rejoice with you now. Great are the wonders of the Eternal, today, as they were a thousand years ago! Praise His name!'

All stood. Skovronnek's daughters, the children, the sons-in-law, and the music salesman had already put on their coats, and were departing. Mendel's friends did not sit down because they had only come to offer congratulations. Smaller than any of them, with his bent back, in his greenish coat, Mendel stood in their midst like a disguised king. He had to stretch himself up to look into their faces.

'I thank you,' he said. 'Without your help I should never have seen this hour. Look at my son!'

He pointed towards him with his hand, as though one of the friends might perhaps have failed to regard Menuchim closely enough. Their eyes felt of the stuff of his suit, of his silk cravat, the pearl, the slender hands, and the ring. Then they said:

'A noble young man! One sees that he is someone special.'

'I have no house,' said Mendel to his son. 'You come to your father and I have no bed to offer you.'

'I want to take you with me, Father,' answered the son. 'But I do not know whether you will go, because today is a feast day.'

'He can go,' they all answered, as though with one mouth.

'I think that I may go with you,' said Mendel. 'I have committed grave sins; God has closed His eyes. I called Him an *ispravnik*. He held His ears. He is so great that our badnesses seem to Him very small. I can go with you.'

They all accompanied Mendel to the car. At this window and that neighbours stood and looked down. Mendel fetched his key, unlocked the shop once more, went into the back room, and took down the red velvet sack from its nail. He blew upon it to disperse the dust, rolled down the iron shutters, locked up, and gave

Skovronnek the key. With the sack in his arms he climbed into the automobile. The motor whirred. The headlights shone. From this window and that voices called: 'Auf wiedersehen, Mendel!'

Mendel Singer grasped Menkes by the arm and said:

'Tomorrow, at prayers, you will announce that I am giving three hundred dollars to the poor. Good-bye!'

And at the side of his son he rode to the Astor Hotel.

XVI

A BENT, PITIABLE figure in a greenish coat, with the red velvet sack under his arm, Mendel Singer entered the lobby, observed the electric light, the blond doorman, the white bust to an unknown God at the entrance of the stairs, and the black Negro who tried to take the sack from him. He entered the lift, and saw himself in its mirror beside his son. He closed his eyes, for he felt dizzy. He was, perhaps, already dead, he thought; he floated in heaven; it would go on like this for ever.

His son took his hand; Mendel walked on the silent carpet, through the long corridor. He only opened his eyes when he finally stood in the room. As was his custom, he immediately stepped to the window. There he saw for the first time America's night close at hand. He saw the reddened heavens, the flaming, sparkling,

dropping, glowing, red, blue, green, silver, golden letters, pictures, and signs. He heard the noisy song of
America, the whistle, the rumble, the ringing, the
screaming, the rattling, the piping, the howling. Across
from the window on which Mendel leaned appeared
every fifth second the broad laughing face of a girl, put
together out of sparkling points of light, between her
parted lips a blinding set of teeth made, seemingly, of a
single piece of molten silver. A foaming ruby-red goblet
swam towards this face, tipped of itself, spilled its contents into the open mouth, and disappeared, only to
return refilled and foaming over with white froth.

It was an advertisement for a new soft drink. Mendel
admired it as the perfected representation of nightly
joys and golden health. He smiled, watched the picture
several times as it came and went, and then turned again
towards the room. There stood a white bed, already
made. Menuchim rested in a deep chair.

'I shall not sleep tonight,' said Mendel. 'You go to
bed. I will sit beside you. In Zuchnow you slept in the
corner, next to the oven.'

'I remember perfectly the day' – began Menuchim,
and laid aside his glasses, and Mendel saw the naked
eyes of his son, and they seemed to him weary and sad –
'I remember perfectly a certain morning. The sun is
very bright and the room is empty. Then you come in.
You lift me up. I sit on a table, and you strike upon a
glass with a spoon. There was a lovely ringing. I wish
that I could reproduce that sound and play it today.
Then you sang. And then the bells began to ring, the

old, old bells. They were like enormous spoons striking upon enormous glasses.'

'Go on, go on!' cried Mendel. He, too, remembered the exact day. It was the day Deborah went out of the house to prepare for the journey to Kapturak.

'From the early days that is all I can recall,' said Menuchim. 'Then the time came when Billes's son-in-law played the violin. I believe that he played every day. When he stopped playing I still heard him. The music went on in my ears, day and night.'

'Go on, go on!' cried Mendel, in the tone in which he had urged his pupils to more zealous effort.

'Then for a long time, nothing. Then one day I saw a great red and blue fire. I lay down on the floor. I crept to the door. Suddenly someone seemed to lift me up and push me. I ran. I was outside. People were standing on the other side of the street. "Fire!" I cried.'

'Go on, go on!' said Mendel.

'I cannot remember the rest. Later people told me that I was sick and unconscious for a long time. After that I remember only the time in Petersburg, a white room, white beds, many children in the beds, an accordion or an organ playing, and I singing with a loud voice in accompaniment. Then the doctor takes me home in his car. A tall blonde woman in a pale-blue dress plays the piano. She stands up. I go to the keys. When I touch them, they sound. Suddenly I see that I can play the songs of the organ and everything that I can sing.'

'Go on, go on!' said Mendel.

'I remember nothing more from the early times

except these few days. I remember my mother. It was warm and soft with her, she had a very deep voice, and her face was big and round, like a whole world.'

'Go on, go on,' said Mendel.

'I cannot remember Miriam, Jonas, or Shemariah at all. I heard about them much later, from Billes's daughter.'

Mendel sighed. 'Miriam,' he repeated. She stood before him, in a golden-yellow shawl, with her blue-black hair, quick and light-footed, a young gazelle. She had his eyes.

'I was a bad father,' said Mendel. 'I treated you badly, and her, too. Now she is lost. No medicine can help her.'

'We will go to her,' said Menuchim. 'Wasn't I healed, Father?'

Yes, Menuchim was right. Man is never content, thought Mendel to himself. Just now he had experienced a miracle, and already he wanted another! Wait, wait, Mendel Singer! Only see what has become of Menuchim, a cripple! Slender are his hands, wise are his eyes, soft are his cheeks.

'Go to sleep, Father,' said the son.

He sat upon the floor and drew off Mendel Singer's old boots. He looked at the soles, which were torn, with broken edges. He looked at the yellow patched tops, the roughened shafts, the holes in the socks, the ragged trousers. He undressed the old man and laid him in bed.

Then he left the room, took a book from a trunk, and returned to his father, sat down in the easy-chair

[Handwritten margin note:] Mendel goes from being someone who is closed off to someone full of desire expecting another miracle — Mendel becomes a presence of hope in the world.

beside the bed, lighted the little green lamp, and began to read. Mendel pretended to sleep. He peeped through a narrow little crack between his lids. His son laid the book aside, and said:

'You are thinking of Miriam, Father! We will visit her. I shall get another doctor. They will heal her. She is still young. Go to sleep.'

Mendel closed his eyes, but he did not sleep. He thought of Miriam, heard the strange noises of the world, felt through his closed eyelids the brightness of the night skies. He did not sleep, but he felt well. He rested. With his head awake he lay bedded in sleep and awaited the morning.

His son prepared a bath for him, dressed him, set him in an automobile. They rode for a long time, through noisy streets. They left the city. They came to a long, wide road, on the edges of which stood budding trees. The motor hummed brightly. Mendel's beard waved in the wind. He was silent.

'Do you want to know where we are going, Father?' asked the son.

'No,' answered Mendel. 'I do not want to know. Wherever you go is well.'

And they reached a world where the sands were yellow, the wide ocean blue, and all the houses white. Mendel Singer sat upon the terrace of one of these houses, before a small white table. He drank a golden-brown tea. Upon his bent back shone the first warm sun of the year. Robins hopped around them, and their sisters piped before the terrace. The waves of the sea splashed upon the strand with a soft, regular beat. A few white clouds stood in the pale-blue sky. Under this sky it was possible for Mendel to think that Jonas might be found again, and Miriam come home, 'in all the land no woman so fair,' he quoted, silently, to himself. He himself, Mendel Singer, would have a good death, after many years, surrounded by grandchildren, 'old and full of days,' as was written of Job. He felt a curious and forbidden desire to lay aside his old cap of silk rep, and feel the sun upon his old skull. And for the first time in his life, Mendel Singer voluntarily uncovered his head, as he had only done in public offices, and in his bath. The few kinky hairs upon his bald head were moved by a gentle spring wind as though they had been rare and tender plants.

Thus Mendel Singer greeted the world.

And a gull, like a silver shot from heaven, flew under the awning of the terrace. Mendel watched its headlong flight, and its shadowy white wake in the blue air.

Then the son said: 'Next week we go to San Francisco. On the way back we play for ten days in Chicago. I think, Father, that in four weeks we can return to Europe.'

'Miriam?'

'I shall see her today, and talk with the doctors. Everything will be all right, Father. Perhaps we can take her with us. Perhaps she will get well in Europe.'

They went back to the hotel. Mendel went into his son's room. He was tired.

'Lie down on the sofa; sleep a little,' said the son. 'I shall be back in two hours.'

218

Mendel lay down obediently. He knew where his son was going. He was going to his sister. He was a wonderful man, his son. Blessing rested upon him. He would make Miriam well.

Mendel caught sight of a big photograph in a brown frame, upon the little dressing-table.

'Give me that picture!' he begged.

He looked at it a long time. He saw a blonde young woman in a light-coloured dress, light as the day, and she sat in a garden through which the wind walked, moving the sprays at the edges of flower beds. Two children, a girl and a boy, stood beside a little carriage with a donkey hitched to it.

'God bless her,' said Mendel.

The son went out. The father rested on the sofa, laying the photograph gently down beside him. His tired eyes wandered through the room, to the window.

From the depths of his couch he could see a broken bit of cloudless sky. He took the picture up again. That was his daughter-in-law, Menuchim's wife; those were his grandchildren, Menuchim's children. When he looked at the girl closely, he thought he saw a childhood picture of Deborah. Deborah was dead. Perhaps with strange otherworldly eyes she saw the miracle from the other side. With gratitude, Mendel remembered the young warmth which he had once delighted in, her red cheeks, her half-open eyes, which had shone in the darkness of their love nights like narrow, luring lights. Dead Deborah!

He stood up, pushed a chair to the sofa, set the

picture on the chair, and lay down again. As his eyes
slowly closed, they took with them into sleep the whole
gay blueness of the sky and the faces of the new children. Beside them arose out of the brown background
the portraits of Miriam and Jonas. Mendel fell asleep.
And he rested from the burden of his happiness, and
the greatness of the miracle.

Afterword

Joseph Roth's boss at the *Frankfurter Zeitung*, Friedrich Traugott Gubler, used to say, half-jokingly, that Roth should always be sad; the sadder he was, the better he wrote. You could say that Roth's seventh novel, *Job* (which was serialized in the *Frankfurter* in September and October 1930), was – happy ending and all – the first of his sad books. To that point they had been mutinous, enigmatic, angry, satirical: resolutely unaccommodated in the post-war world. Then – it's no disgrace – the world defeated him, life defeated him. After 1930, they are all sad.

Not that Roth had to try to follow Gubler's prescription. Sad things kept happening to him, and increasingly only sad things. After the early and unlooked-for zenith of his life in 1925, when – thirty, married, published and employed – he saw Paris and saw Marseilles and the rest of the French Midi, and had a vision of a multi-ethnic, inclusive, catholic Europe all under one sun, it was downhill from there. The *Frankfurter Zeitung*, which had given him France as a correspondent's posting, took it away again, and gave it instead to the Nationalist Friedrich Sieburg. (This wasn't a career reverse, it was a moral and epistemological catastrophe.) Roth was bought off with a tour to Russia – inspected by H.G. Wells and Walter Benjamin and Sinclair Lewis and André Gide and Egon Erwin Kisch and pretty much everyone who was anyone in Western intellectual circles in the 1920s and 1930s. He wrote *Juden auf Wanderschaft*, his short book about Eastern Jews. (This was where he did some of the legwork for *Job* – the *shtetl*, the ghetto, the drama of military call-up, the intensification of westward migration following the war, the 'uncle in America' and the Jewish fear of sailing.) Roth wrote a series of articles on Germany and discouraging developments there, rapidly becoming allergic to the place, aesthetically, politically, humanly. He spent far more time than he could have wanted to in Frankfurt, in the way that a representative for a failing firm hangs around head office, in the hope perhaps of intercepting the last plum job – or the terminating cable. He tried his luck with a rival paper – a Rightist rag of all things, the *Münchener Neueste Nachrichten*. Then he fell out of love with newspapers altogether, and tried to manage without them (difficult with his overheated personal economy), compensating with the accelerated production of books, and for the first time in his life they failed: *The Silent Prophet, Perlefter, Strawberries,* something spun off from *Right and Left,* all were rejected or remained fragmentary, or both. 'Must finish novel in three days. Must finish novel in three days. Must finish novel in three days' – the post-it inevitably wound up in the pages of the manuscript, and the manuscript was snootily returned.

The urgency was driven by checks, by a darkening politics, by simply growing older – but above all by a sense, gradually focused to a certainty, that all was not well with Friedl, his wife of seven years, whom he describes worriedly as 'physically not up to a life at my side'. He blamed himself and the instability and unsuitability of that life: no home, no children, nothing settled; just hotel rooms, railway compartments, absences and deadlines. He hoped against hope that what was ailing Friedl and causing her outbreaks of obscene and eccentric and unpredictable behaviour was physiological and physical and remediable. He put her on a regimen of raw liver and blood soup, and – yes – had her taken to a wonder rabbi. He himself took to drink. Somewhere at the very back of his mind, Roth must have thought of his own father, Nahum (whom he had never seen, and who died when he was a boy), losing his mind. On 2nd September 1929 – his uncommented thirty-fifth birthday – the dark wood closed around him. This instinctively most discreet of correspondents abruptly lowered his guard. To Stefan Zweig, whom he had only recently met for the first time, in May 1929, he wrote, from Berlin:

'Since we last saw each other, a lot of very grim things have happened. My wife was taken to the psychiatric hospital at Westend [in Berlin] in a very bad state, and for some weeks I've been unable to write a line, and compel myself to scribble just enough to keep body and soul together. I'll spare you any more detailed account of my condition. The word "torment" has just acquired a very real and substantial content, and the feeling of being surrounded by misfortune as by high black walls doesn't leave me for a second. I had hoped to be able to give you my manuscript in pleasanter circumstances. I am sending it to you now under the very worst and most grievous.'

The manuscript in question was that of *Job*, widely regarded as Roth's most perfect book (along with its 1932 follow-up and not-at-all *semblable*, *The Radetzky March*); the book that first brought his fiction a wider readership; the book of his that was first translated into English (a vivid and loyal translation), by Dorothy Thompson, the renowned American journalist and anti-Fascist and then-wife of Sinclair Lewis; and the book that Stefan Zweig would keep returning to ten years later, in 1939, in his obituary for his gifted, exorbitant and now prematurely deceased friend. One has to think of Roth in these months fighting against misfortune in his life and writing a miracle in a book, because as he wisely says in *Job*: 'he who has had no misfortunes does not believe in miracles', only to begin a new paragraph and to go on: 'Yes, and those who have misfortunes do not believe in miracles.' All the time he was in anguish and guilt about Friedl (who was eventually diagnosed with schizophrenia, institutionalized outside Vienna, and put to death by the Nazis in 1940), he was writing the culpable neglect of little Menuchim, the nympho-maniac self-abandon of Miriam, and the dramatic overnight ageing of Deborah. (Roth gave instructions that Friedl was on no account to read *Job*: he didn't want her to be influenced by what befalls Miriam.) The reader can only marvel at a scene like this one, where extreme of distress is matched by a kind of methodical beauty, equal parts chronometry and colour, fairytale and observation:

> 'Suddenly Deborah began, very slowly, with stroking fingers, to rumple her hair. She pulled one strand after another over her face, which was pale and immobile as plaster. One after another she rent the strands of hair, one after another, in the same tempo in which, outside, the flakes were falling. Two, then three, white islands appeared amidst her hair, a few spots the size of a dollar where the naked scalp showed, and a few tiny drops of red blood. No one moved. The clock ticked, the snow fell, and Deborah quietly tore out her hair. (p. 152)'

Roth's predecessor, Heinrich Heine – they were both Jewish fugitives from Germany, to Paris, and both unusually clever and unusually rounded writers – wrote:

'aus den grossen Schmerzen mach' ich die kleinen Lieder' (out of the big pains/sorrows/griefs I make the little songs). Roth didn't do self-deprecation, but he had a similar interest in this sort of alchemy. It is hard not to think that Roth didn't write his *Job* as an offer, or challenge, to Fate.

The Austrian Emperor Franz Joseph appears in *The Radetzky March*, but there is no role for God in *Job*: nor is there any of the bold rhetorical and theological ping-pong of the scriptural Book of Job. Roth's Job – his 'entirely commonplace Jew', Mendel Singer – is there purely to suffer and to endure suffering. At most he is there as a sort of lightning-conductor for a miracle, but let it be a miracle in Roth's life, and not the formally necessary but uncertain and offstage one here. Roth's concern is not with religion or theology. He is not inter-ested in establishing a morality for God; his focus is on the human world. Prayer interests him, if at all, as absence, as a form of ritual, as unworldly speech or even as a disciplined form of male truancy (a first cousin, if you will, to newspaper articles, or novels), while a higher authority is a plot device and a fond hypothesis. (Interestingly, the last thing he wrote, *The Legend of the Holy Drinker*, offers a not dissimilar account of a Catholic miracle.) Roth's biographer, David Bronsen, writes cor-rectly and acutely: 'Roth, who was capable of serious rebellion and serious despair, could not quite take him-self seriously in his existential leap of faith, he was too sceptical towards his own desire to believe.' In the fable of *Job* it is the want of earthly justice that drives Roth, rather than any particular faith in its superior, celestial form. To a friend who pointed out the difference between his character and the biblical Job, who keeps his faith and never loses God, he replied sombrely: 'My Job doesn't find Him.' His Singer can neither earn grace, nor curse God. He has a telephone in his hand, but it may be a child's plastic telephone. Perhaps it was the failure of his book to produce an actual miracle that led Roth to turn against it – which is unusual for him, he wasn't Kafka – so quickly and virulently; before it had even come out. In September 1930, he was writing to Zweig: 'Thank you for reading *Job* once more. I for my part find it superfluous to have written it. I have no ties to it any more. I am tired of it, or I am simply tired.' It cost too much. And it didn't do what he so desperately and forlornly hoped it would.

Roth's great achievement in *Job* is a curt, pictorial, but discreetly intelligent prose. His fearlessly short, stubby, sprung sentences run the gamut from folkloric glass-painting ('Miriam would comb the white feathers out of her black hair') to poetry ('Her eyes were dry and empty, like two little pieces of glass') to aphorism ('One is not healed in strange hospitals'). Almost like a feminine influence, bright, balancing adjectives consort with rudimentary nouns and mostly simple, functional verbs. One rarely finds 'white' without 'black', 'silver' without 'gold', 'red' without 'blue'. Light and rain, sun and moon, clocks and seasons, horses and fields are recurring presences. Little runs of

sentences are arranged in exquisite cinematic
sequences:

'The narrow winding streets were covered with a
silver-grey mud. The high boots of the passersby
sank into it, and the cartwheels disappeared to the
hubs. Rain veiled the fields, dispersed the smoke
over the isolated huts, pounded with endless
patience everything firm that it struck – the limestone which here and there grew out of the earth
like a white tooth; the sawed-up logs at the edges of
the road; the aromatic boards piled one upon
another before the entrance to the saw-mill; the
shawl on Deborah's head; and the woollen blanket
under which Menuchim's head lay buried. No
drop must wet him.' (p. 11)

It seems the human is menaced equally by dilution, dis-
appearance and hard edges: one wonders if wool alone
can be enough to shield it. Roth's scenic presentation
allows a careful, diligent humour at times, where the
little puns on 'still' and 'float' seem to drift along on the
inevitable, irreverent current of Bible-slaying oral grati-
fication; the compromised embarrassment of the three
older children is exquisite:

'But sometimes nothing would still the infant's
desire to whimper and cry. His voice croaked over
the voices of the twelve studying children, an ugly
and profane noise above the Bible's holy verses.

Deborah stood on a footstool and lifted the infant down. White, swollen, and colossal, her breast flowed from her open blouse and drew the glances of the boys irresistibly. All present seemed to suckle at Deborah. Her own three older children stood about her, jealous and greedy; the room became still. One heard the smacking of the infant.' (p. 7)

At other times the short sentences teeter into a more oblique kind of comedy:

'Then it was quiet. One heard the ticking of the clock. Through Venetian blinds the golden light of late afternoon shone. The papers rustled. Once the official meditated, gazed into the air, and suddenly swatted a fly with his hand. He held the tiny animal in his huge fist, opened his hand cautiously, pulled off a wing, then another, and watched for a second how the crippled insect crept about the desk.' (p. 88)

And what function does this terrible official have, with his unpleasant predilection for the immobilising of small, helpless creatures? Why, wouldn't you know it, he works in emigration. The grim joke here does what the pictorial does elsewhere: provides a little excess, a little commentary, some sympathetic orchestration; it speaks in an image. As the family is waiting to take ship in Bremerhaven, they are confined to barracks. Themselves on their way to freedom, they are ominously

229

JOSEPH ROTH

unfree: 'It was forbidden to make tea. They had gone to sleep with dry mouths. But a Polish barber had offered Miriam red bon-bons. Miriam went to sleep with a great sticky candy-drop in her mouth.' Again, a sudden burst of colour, of sweetness, of eroticism, of psychology (remember the white feathers being combed out of the black hair, another expression of the bright, attractive, bed- and man-orientated girl: 'Another Cossack, thought Mendel').

The Russian part of the book has generally had more praise than the American, but the thick-lined colourful style does not disgrace Roth in the New World (who never made it to America, but who considered it part of his mythology, had referred to it already in *Hotel Savoy* and some of the stories, and had clearly managed to glean up-to-date information about the Lower East Side from various sources, among them Dorothy Thompson). It is in *Job*, for instance, that there is the earliest description I know of that haunting and arcane feature of the modern city, 'the regularly recurrent, silver finger of a great searchlight which swept the sky as if desperately searching for God' (p. 141). There isn't perhaps the pure intelligence and dry Zenoesque comedy of Roth's American section in *The Wandering Jews* (where the Jews make it no further than quarantine on Ellis Island, peering through wire fencing at the Statue of Liberty and wondering whether it is she or they who have been confined), but there are still any number of other droll and plausible touches. Thus, Mendel has a healthy fear of the American wisecrack: 'Already he was afraid that one

230

of those American stories was coming, which all the world seemed to find funny, and which Mendel could find no pleasure in at all.' Mendel and his émigré acquaintance set up a sort of counter-America within America, a protest not out of anger or dissent, but difference, bewilderment and quite possibly gratitude. It was in America, 'where everybody hurried', that Mendel learns to walk slowly. In another one of the book's dreamy, unforgettable scenes – as often, it seems to be neither day nor night, and only the adjectives are really awake – he looks out of the window:

> 'It still snowed a little – slow, lazy, damp flakes. The Jews, with open umbrellas waving over their heads, began their promenade up and down. More and more came. They walked in the middle of the street; the last white scraps of snow melted under their feet; it looked as though they had to walk up and down by order of the authorities, until the snow had entirely disappeared.' (p. 149)

The sardonic litany of American virtues and perspectives, facts and aspirations – the categories are so fluid as to be interchangeable – is perhaps to be expected from Roth, the satirist of the 1920s (though one notes how absurdly little has changed in the 90 years since: substitute Steve Jobs for Edison, and it's bang up to date!):

> 'Americans were healthy, their women pretty, sport was important, time was money, poverty was a

crime, riches a service, virtue was half of success, and belief in oneself the whole of it, dancing was hygienic, roller-skating a duty, charity was an investment, anarchism a crime, strikers were enemies of mankind, agitators instruments of the Devil, modern machinery a gift of God, Edison the world's greatest genius.' (p. 139)

But against that, how wholly unexpected and interesting and subtle is this little weakness – or shyness – on the part of Mac: 'For it was characteristic of Mac that he would brag with enthusiasm of things which were total fabrications, and remain entirely silent about things which he really accomplished' (p. 117).

Job is a 'lost leader', a glimpse of what might have been if Roth had been spared in 1930, and in 1939, to take his great and shapely gifts and exercise them in America, like, say, Isaac Bashevis Singer, his junior by just ten years. But it wasn't to be; Roth's world is the old world, the one we broke, and have missed desperately ever since.

Michael Hofmann
Gainesville–Glasgow
February 2013

Keep in touch with
Granta Books:

Visit grantabooks.com to discover more.

GRANTA